Uncommon
DENOMINATOR

A Jake Quinn Mystery

By Jackson Klaiber

Outskirts Press Inc.
Denver, CO

Uncommon Denominator: A Jake Quinn Mystery
All Rights Reserved
Copyright © 2004 Jeffrey Lundy

Outskirts Press
http://www.outskirtspress.com

ISBN: 1-932672-46-X

Outskirts Press and the "OP" logo are trademarks belonging to Outskirts Press, Inc.

Printed in the United States of America

Dedicated to two Jakes, Carrie, Jay, and a Brady.

Chapter One

——

A lawyer represents maybe one elephant like Alex Beckett in a career. I knew it. And so did he.

So I had no one to blame but myself starting the week with a four hour drive to Corning, New York. Alex had personally called the office the week before and my secretary, the fair haired pit bull Eva Petrovic, had set up a meeting with Mrs. Elizabeth Frampton, explained as a "possible widow." The law is a bit funny about that: to be a widow the husband should be dead, which was the reason for the meeting. Apparently Elizabeth Frampton was having trouble convincing her insurance company that the dearly departed was in fact "departed."

Corning was one of the last company towns in the east, Hershey, Pennsylvania maybe the other. Everything in Hershey is "chocolate", even the streetlights. Everything in Corning was "glass", even the restaurants. The "Glass Onion Bistro", a small restaurant across from the Stuben Glass Works, is where the widow Frampton instructed me to meet her. Arriving early for the noon lunch, I reviewed the insurance company letter Eva had efficiently placed in a folder. Not a lot of facts. A boat sank and Mrs. Frampton's husband was supposed to have been aboard. Glancing through the letter, I caught the waitress directing a petite blond to the booth. Maybe in her late thirties, she had a confident walk, stylish conservative pants suit with a white open blouse and clever smile. Within a few feet of the table she readily extended her hand and, part declaration, part query, with a noticeable British accent, said:

"Attorney Jake Quinn?"

Rising and accepting her firm handshake, I said: "Mrs. Frampton, glad to meet you." I motioned for her to have a seat with a "Please."

She sat down, placed her shoulder strap purse and cloth attaché beside her, turned to the waitress, saying with familiar tone: "I'll have lemonade, Judy."

Leaning forward, pressing against the edge of the table making sure significant cleavage preceded her speaking, Elizabeth Frampton wasted no time in getting to the point of the meeting:

"Mr. Quinn, I have never had occasion to need the services of an American solicitor, or barrister for that matter. Mr. Beckett recommended you to discuss my insurance problem. Apparently, he has faith in your abilities. And discretion."

She paused expecting some affirmation. I simply nodded in a positive manner.

"What kind of work do you do for Alex?" She said.

"I don't think it would *bode* well for you or Mr. Beckett's idea of discretion if I told you." Bode? You unconsciously insert such words when around Brits.

"What did Alex tell you?" I said.

"Not a lot, which should not surprise you." she said, as the waitress brought over a lemonade. "Just that he trusted you and thought you could handle the insurance company. He assured me you had worked for his company resolving insurance claims. Have you read the insurance letter?"

I picked up my "marked up" copy while at the same time she pulled up her attaché and withdrew a manila folder, with the words: "CNI Correspondence", neatly typed across the top. She placed her original on top of the folder and said with a firm demeanor:

"Where do I stand with CNI?"

The letter from CNI, Continental National Insurance, was authored by Timothy Fruntz, Senior Claims Adjustor, referencing "George Frampton" and was not a denial, so much as a "further investigation warranted." The policy was for one hundred thousand dollars. I said:

"CNI has no intention of paying in the near future, if that's what you want to know. The letter was sent to prevent a bad faith claim later. What was your impression when you talked to the adjuster?"

"He was very sympathetic, asking a few questions concerning what I knew about the accident, which I told him was not much, and he said he would keep me informed. He made a point of saying it was life insurance, and since they didn't have a death certificate, it was difficult to pay. He wanted a copy of our marriage certificate. They also were investigating the cause of the yacht sinking because they had a subrogation right. What does that mean Mr. Quinn?"

Feeling she already knew, but giving the benefit of the doubt: "Well, it means that if CNI pays you the life insurance money they can try to recover that payment from whoever caused the accident. Do you have any idea what caused the accident?"

"Not really. The adjuster's letter is as much as I know. My husband was on Alex's fishing yacht off Cat Cay in the Bahamas and it sank. I wasn't there."

Before I had time to follow-up with any questions, she said: "Look. Alex insisted I meet with you. I did. He said if anyone could get me the money it was you. But I hope he is right about you. I would really like to have this wrapped up quickly. To be honest, no offense, but I would rather have had a city lawyer."

I catalogued but ignored the *honest* insult: "It may take some time Mrs. Frampton."

Smiling, but this time with a cut: "I'm sure Alex would like it better if it didn't."

She got up, picked up her purse and attaché and headed out the door. She looked back, making sure I was looking at her: "You have my number. Put the check on my bill."

She was out the door as the waitress brought me the check. As I put the money for the check on the table I said to her: "Have you known Elizabeth long."

"Liz. Not real long. She's been coming in here regular for maybe six months, a year."

"Shame about her husband." I said.

Wiping the table, not looking up, she said: "Yeah, someone said she lost her husband. I never met him."

I paid the bill and did the tourist drive though Corning, viewing the old mansions, figuring I wouldn't be back anytime soon, if ever. I was wrong about that.

Chapter Two

—

On my drive back to the office that afternoon I cell phoned Tim Fruntz, the adjuster, to talk about the case. Found out he was no longer involved. Attorney Gordan Marks, of Peters and Marks, out of Pittsburgh, had taken over the case. It seemed odd to get the lawyers involved before a shot was even fired and he didn't disagree. Calling Eva, I asked her to see if Marks was available to meet with me, which I doubted. I also told her to phone Bryan Kaypro, an investigator of sorts in Pittsburgh, and tell him I would be emailing him some information.

When I got to the office Eva had arranged a two o'clock meeting the next day with Marks at the Duquesne Club, mentioning she was as surprised as I was that Marks was willing to "fit me in". She also set up a noon meeting with Bryan at the Oyster House. I wasn't thrilled about another road trip, but there was no use complaining to Eva.

Eva had been with me for ten years and she had accomplished "the switch": I seemed to work for her now. Somewhere in her thirties, blond and in constant mortal combat with Weight Watchers, she attracted her fair share of men. They willingly lined up to be pulverized like a car crusher. I feared her wrath, as did, fortunately, most clients.

The "firm" was just me and Eva and was located in a civil war era Italiate style mansion on the outskirts of Punxsutawney, Pennsylvania. My office and Eva's were on the first floor, the top two my residence. The practice was composed of the usual fare, occasionally venturing on a Quixote quest for truth, justice and the American way. Having an Alex and his vast array of companies to represent on occasion paid the heating bills.

The next morning I drove to Pittsburgh for the luncheon with

Bryan. I parked at the garage near Kaufman's Department Store, walked the two blocks to Oyster House at Market Square, and found a vacant table under the life-size faded poster of Rockie Marciano. On the tile walls hung small photos of celebrities, some local, some national, all who passed through the swinging door. Behind me hung dozens of fading black and whites of Miss America contestants on the beach at Atlantic City. The original owner had been married to the 1940 Miss Pennsylvania.

Leaning against the aluminum bar stood young and old professionals wrestling fish sandwiches, catching their handsome reflections in the bar length mirror. Interspersed was an assortment of characters, classified as "not dangerous to themselves or others". They no longer needed to look in the mirror. Craziness quiets the ego.

The waitress, Dorie, less than an octogenarian, but not by much, short, getting shorter each year, in a white button down blouse, black slacks, apron, white hair pushed up, took my order for an "Iron', an unlikable beer I'm compelled to drink when in Pittsburgh. Bryan strolled in as if caught between physics classes: five-two in height, short dark hair, unpressed khakis, a Steelers jersey, and a brown safari jacket. A Pittsburgh geek: Steelers fanatic with a Carnegie Mellon University computer wiz living inside. Bryan lists his occupation as Cybersultant, CEO of "Techtives." Money is not an object, or shouldn't be, as Bryan had cashed in on a CMU developed internet before the dot com bust. I handled the buy out, referred to me by Gordan Marks, as Bryan wanted someone outside the city and Marks didn't want the contact going to a downtown competitor. Bryan now did consulting and internet investigations for cyber companies, insurers and law firms. Business was brisk.

I kicked the chair out so Bryan could sit down, saying: "How's Nicole."

"Fine. She said to say hi. I can't believe we're eating here instead of the Edison. She was pissed. Eva's doing no doubt."

Nicole was Bryan's voluptuous twenty-five year old live-in who worked as a stripper at the Edison Hotel on Liberty Avenue. With an IQ higher than Bryan's, she also worked for him part time doing computer research. Bryan and Nicole had been house guests of mine several times and Eva failed to intimidate Nicole, much to our delight. I said:

"Don't blame Eva, I knew if we went there I wouldn't make my meeting with Marks."

Dorie came back bringing Bryan an Iron and we ordered the mandatory fish sandwiches.

"Did you get my email?" I said. The email gave him as much information as I had with the insurance letter attached. I asked Bryan to make inquiries, discreet or otherwise, to see if there was any street talk about the case. Pittsburgh is a very small town. Bryan usually had great instincts in obtaining insurance information, you just had to be careful not to ask for sources.

Pulling out my email from his dirty forty dollar blue cloth briefcase, he said: "Yes, I did. Interesting. Still kissing Alex Beckett's ass."

The universal hand gesture was my physical response, the verbal: "That's why you're a bad influence on Nicole."

He took a drink of his Iron: "Plenty of shop talk about this one. Continental shopped the case around law firms, looking for the best hourly rate."

"They're shopping a case with a hundred thousand exposure? I don't think so."

"I don't either. If they hired Marks, there are seven figures somewhere. They specifically asked Tom Graham to work on it knowing Marks doesn't do front line work. Graham's the Burgh's new golden boy for insurance defense."

Graham. Everyone hates lawyers, and then there are lawyers even the lawyers hate. A monkey could do insurance defense work and Graham was their new baboon.

I said: "What else?"

"I'm going to need time and facts to do you much good. All CNI's insurance computers have new complicated fire walls. It's going to take time to get break in."

"Christ! Don't tell me stuff like that."

"You asked."

"Look, after I meet with Marks I'll get back in touch. Try to keep your invasion of privacy to a minimum."

"Ok boss."

We finished our sandwiches and beer, talking sports and megabits. He walked with me the several blocks up to the Duquesne Club. He was going on to the Edison's Art Rooney Room, maybe catch Nicole, and her friend Jean, in their duo. Bamboo curtains and a neon moon, it gets good late in the Rooney Room.

Chapter Three

The Duquesne Club is nestled on a narrow one way street between old brick skyscrapers and the historic Trinity Church. Until the late sixties, doing business in Pittsburgh began at the Duquesne Club. But golf memberships to Oakmont and the Field Club are now a better use of corporate networking dollars and the Duquesne Club has become an historic backdrop for lunches. Mellon, Frick and Carnegie no doubt rolled in their graves when one of their billiard rooms was converted to a Fitness Center.

Other than Groundhog Day, top hats are an anomaly in Western Pennsylvania, but the doorman at the Duquesne Club still sported one, along with his black tie and red tails. I walked up the short steep steps he patrolled, nodded and passed through the oak and mahogany entrance. On my right two gentlemen sat in the billiard room smoking cigars. I stood in the hallway thinking how out of character it was for Gordan Marks to meet on a case before a representation letter was sent. A meeting with Marks was more sophisticated, more intellectual shuffling. Factual nuance is slowly incorporated into the conversation, leveraged to maximum benefit. Final positions are rarely laid on the table.

In a few minutes Marks, with Thomas Graham in tow cruised in. Marks greeted me with a smile and firm hand shake, dressed in a well cut Hickey-Freeman, blue shirt with white collar. Marks was in his mid fifties but forty looking if you had to guess. Graham, early forties, looking fifty, dressed about the same, but the demeanor of a differential junior partner.

Marks said: "Jake, good to see you. You know Tom Graham, don't you?"

"Yeah, we've worked across the aisle." I shook Graham's

weak hand and said to Marks: "Good to see you Gordan."

"Let's get a table. Are you in hurry?"

"No." I said. Marks never mentioned if he was under a time constraint as that was to be assumed.

As we walked through the small atrium to the dining area, Marks and I swapped a recent courtroom war story while Graham followed, letting me sense, but not Marks, his irritation at his secondary role. It felt like walking through the high school halls talking to the head cheerleader with her boyfriend following. My animosity to Graham was mostly professional, although maybe personal, as he was a pompous ass. Everyone basks in winning; he took pleasure in the other attorney losing. I was convinced, but couldn't prove, several years before he had conspired with a whining University of Pittsburgh surgeon to alter medical records in a malpractice case.

We took our seats, ordered our lunches, and after some more causal conversation, Marks got to the point: "Jake, I was glad to get your call. I'll be honest with you Jake, CNI is a new client and we're not up to speed on all their policies. We plan to keep them, and don't want any screw ups, even though the case is small. But because of our firm's past relationship with you we wanted to get together and see if we could compare notes. Tom met with the head of their Loss Committee. If the case is going to settle, we want to do it quickly."

Turning to Tom he said: "Tom, give Jake your impression of that meeting."

Graham looked vaguely perplexed that Marks would direct him to give me his "impressions", but he dutifully opened a file from his briefcase, moving his drink to the side and said to me:

"As you know, this might involve the Merritt Boat Company. Merritt's a family owned corporation out of Florida and fabricates the most expensive sports fishing yachts in the world. They're the Rolex of their industry and it's all about reputation. They have never had a successful claim against them."

Graham paused to make sure I absorbed the last sentence. I saw no need to tell Graham I was well aware of Merritt, having been to their facility the year before when Alex started construction of his new boat.

Graham continued: "The fishing yacht that went down was on a trial run and has not been recovered. Your client's husband George Frampton is missing. The captain and first mate survived."

Graham appeared to be ready to continue reading or summarizing his file, but paused while the waitress brought drinks. Before he could speak again, Marks said:

"Jake, that's about all we have at this point. Glad to give you whatever we can along the way."

That was glorious bullshit. Marks wanted control from the beginning and didn't want the adjuster doing anything further. Adjuster's notes and interviews were subject to discovery. A savvy lawyer like Marks would make sure everything from this point forward was cloaked in the attorney-client privilege.

My response was scripted lawyer talk. Looking hopefully sincere, but perfectly disingenuous, I said: "I appreciate that Gordan. I'm sure if I find out anything, you'll be the first to know."

"Good. We have an understanding. Let's have another drink and talk about something important. How's your golf game?"

We talked about Marks single digit handicap and the promises to play Oakmont which never materialize. We had another drink and I said I had to go. Graham said he would walk me out while Marks took a call. When we got to the front entrance, Graham said coldly:

"Let me tell you something. If I can help it Quinn, you'll never see a fucking dime."

I stared at him a few seconds, grinned and said: "You know cowboy, I ought to just kick your god damn ass right here."

"Very mature." He said and walked away.

The doorman heard me and as I handed him a ten dollar tip, ready to head back to the garage and my car, he said with a smile: "Sir, if you do kick Mr. Graham's arrogant behind, give him one for me, will you?" I nodded and handed him another ten.

Chapter Four

——

Leaving the parking garage by way of Grant Street, I checked my cell voice mail. Eva had left two messages. A reminder that the office line of credit was maxed and Dean McDonald called. I was to make sure I called him back before I left Pittsburgh.

Dean was Alex's ex son-in-law, having married his only daughter, Trina. Dean still worked for the company and oversaw the Pompano Beach office complex, mainly collecting rent. His duties included overseeing Alex's business toys, principally the jet and the fishing yachts. Trina ran most of the companies under Alex's umbrella corporation, registered as Alex Beckett Enterprises, Inc., but logoed and known as A.B.E. Although Dean and Trina had been divorced for more than ten years, I was sheepish talking to Dean as I had a more than business relationship with Trina on and off after they separated. I had not been with Trina for several years.

Crossing the Allegheny River on Route 28 North just past the Heinz factory I called A.B.E. in Florida. Bonnie, the receptionist and de facto manager, put me through to Dean.

"Dean. Jake Quinn."

"Jake Quinn. How's the weather?"

"Fine. I'm sure it's better where you are Dean."

"Good. Good."

A long pause, so I said: "Dean, you still on the line?"

"Oh, yeah. Alex wants to send his plane up to pick you up in Pittsburgh or DuBois. What do you think?"

"Is there a choice?"

"Not really. What do you want me to tell the pilot, Jefferson County Airport or Pittsburgh?"

"Jefferson would make it a lot easier for me."

"Good. Good. I'll call him now. He's only been in the air about a half hour."

"What? He's already on his way?"

"You know Alex. The plane should be there in about two and a half, three hours. See ya, Jake."

That gave me just enough time to get back, grab a bag, and make the half hour drive to the Jefferson County Airport. Presumptive on Alex's part? No. Few turn down jetting privately anywhere. Elephants nod and it gets done.

Two and half hours later I was checking through the minimal security at the Jefferson County Airport watching Alex's new Cessna land. Originally a private airport to haul Brockway Glass, now Owens-Illinois, executives, it had seen better times when coal was king and glass Coke bottles were more than flea market memorabilia. Not designed for jets, pilots had the feeling of landing on an aircraft carrier in the woods, without the hook cables.

Alex's Cessna made its drop landing and taxied to the terminal in front of the Over the Moon Café. Alex's pilot got out, grabbing my bag while motioning me up the steps over the roar of the engines. I climbed inside, waiving to the co-pilot, no one else on board. The pilot did his outside visual inspection, came in, and pressed the button to raise and seal the door. Before he took his seat he handed me an envelope and we were in the air five minutes later on our way to the Gold Coast's finest tarmac: West Palm.

The envelope contained a letter to Merritt Boat Company from Meyers Yacht Security out of Bahia-Mar, Florida. There was no note or explanation on who obtained the letter, but my guess was that Merritt probably sent it over to Dean to keep him informed. The relationship Merritt had with yacht customers was personal and exclusive to the well-heeled. Merritt's niche was servicing the high end sports fisherman. Fast boats, capable of the long haul to Venezuela or wherever else the last of the bill fish dwell. When Merritt builds a boat there are no written contracts or price quotes. Just an occasional billing statement for maybe a thousand dollar custom toilet seat or a half million dollar CAT diesel. Merritt had no outstanding account receivables.

Meyers Yacht Security was a private investigative firm that mainly tracked missing yachts. Piracy of expensive yachts at sea around the Bahamas was a lucrative trade, either for drug runners or money tight millionaires needing to even the balance sheet on all those insurance dollars paid over the years. Meyers had a special knack of finding boats where the crew miraculously survived but the boat didn't. Apparently, Mr. Frampton didn't have a miracle in reserve.

The letter was an overview of the investigation to date. The keys had been delivered to Alex a week before, and Art "OB" O'Brian, Alex's full time captain, piloted it to the Bahaman Cat Cay islands off the Florida coast where Alex maintained a home. OB was to run a series of sea trials and tests, check under the bow, and kick the rudder. When that was completed, Quiet Tidal, his current yacht, would be "traded in" and the new boat officially registered with the authorities. Dean said Alex was partial to Quiet Tidal, but didn't like the configuration of the ice coolers and seats on the deck. What point is there in owning a three million dollar boat if getting ice cubes was a hassle? Dean confided that he thought the real reason for the new boat was that Alex liked the idea of building a boat, more than owning one. So the new yacht, a slightly bigger fifty-seven foot configuration, would be virtually the same: main cabin, sleeping quarters on the deck below, and then down to the engine and storage in the hull.

OB and Alex had made a few runs the day before the accident and everything checked out except one of the radars. OB was going out the next day with Mike Clontz, the first mate on the Pharaoh, a seventy foot Hercules, usually docked at Cat Cay in the winter. Alex did not maintain a regular first mate unless fishing in Venezuela or Mexico. Clontz, apparently, but this was not clear, had asked Frampton to go along so they had another person to watch the radar screen in the upper pilot console. Frampton also wanted to see Sandy Cay, a nearby island.

Leaving in the morning, the story goes, by noon they were off Sandy Cay, about ten nautical miles from Cat, close to the shelf. The captain was testing the controls and starting to recheck the radar in the tuna tower, when Clontz said he was going below to check the engines. A few minutes later there was a noticeable noise from below, maybe the engine room, the captain could not be certain. He put the controls on auto pilot and was getting down from the tower when suddenly the boat rocked hard to the right. Smoke was now billowing out of the engine room into the main cabin. Clontz rushed out of the main cabin onto the deck, coughing and yelling to get the life raft launched. Clontz said Frampton had an extinguisher and was trying to put out the fire. The captain moved to the bow launching the raft over the side, while Clontz tried to get back into the main cabin. Smoke continued to pour out from the engine and main cabin and the boat was now rapidly sinking. The captain told Clontz to get in the raft and get it far enough away so if the boat rolled the raft would not get caught in the tuna tower. The captain tried to get back through the main cabin to the engine room to below where Frampton was, when the boat suddenly began to dive forward, bow first. OB had no choice but to jump off the back of the deck, into the water. The boat sank to the bottom of the ocean in a matter of seconds, with Frampton still inside. This happened a month ago and neither the boat nor the body had been recovered.

The Bahamians had opened an investigation since it occurred in their waters but no death certificate had been issued. Without the death certificate the insurance company had a stay on paying on the life insurance. Meyers' letter concluded that there was nothing from the records of construction to indicate any mechanical problems. The investigation was on hold until the boat was found and salvaged.

I put the letter back in the envelope as the co-pilot came back to offer a drink and a snack. Nothing more to do for now than sit back and enjoy the high life a couple of hours until we landed in Florida. The pilot was playing Delbert McClinton's "Room to Breath" CD in the background. The co-pilot asked if I needed anything. I asked how to work the leather recliner seat. He pointed out the buttons on the side. I leaned back thinking there are those that say the rich are not really happy. Too much stuff. If asked to provide expert testimony, from my view, there was insufficient evidence to support such a jealous proposition.

Chapter Five

I felt the Florida afternoon heat off the tarmac when I exited the Cessna at West Palm. The pilot got my bag and I made the short walk to the Signature terminal. Signature was a small retro building where the private jet pilots and their corporate clientele checked in and out. Nearby was "Island Air", a two plane operation run by two ex-Navy pilots that provided flights to some of the Bahamian islands, mainly Cat Cay and Bimini.

Cliff Cox was standing beside his single engine "Island Air" Piper, ready for the next leg of my trip to Cat Cay. Dressed in a Captain's shirt, white with shoulder emblems, black narrow tie, contrasted with palm tree printed Bermuda shorts and sneakers, he said:

"Drop your socks, and grab your jock. It's me and you Jake. Good to go, Commander?"

"Sure am."

"I sure could use a Khalik." He said, wiping his forehead.

Khalik was the national beer of the Bahamas, and Cliff and I had downed a few one night at the Compleat Angler in Bimini. He threw my bag in the back seat as I crawled into the co-pilot seat, putting on the headset, and listening while Cliff got clearance from the tower. Cliff taxied out to the runway, the throttles forward, rubbed the head of a small troll doll hanging off the instruments and we were airborne, Miami just visible on the right. I had made this trip many times but not so many to lose the thrill of flying low and fast over the deep blue Atlantic. Banking left, we headed east for the fifty mile, twenty minute flight to Cat Cay.

The Bahamas are a chain of large and small islands, reefs, cays, pronounced most often as "keys". The closest Bahamian land to the Florida shores are the two islands of Cat Cay.

The main island of Cat Cay is a mile and a half long and no more than a couple football fields wide in places. Surrounded by turquoise ocean fading into deep blue outlining the shelves, most of the island is leased from the Bahaman government for private beach homes for the multi millionaire members of the Cat Key Club. The common denominator for admission is the same for all wealthy clubs: money. Bunches.

Walking distance from Number Five green when the tide is out is South Cat. Uninhabited, a couple hundred yards wide, maybe quarter mile long it has a small abandoned lighthouse, but nature had returned South Cat to how Columbus' crew may have seen it: pine wood, iron trees and natural thick thorny vegetation. You could walk the perimeter, but crossing the middle was a tough excursion.

Approaching Cat Cay, Cliff flew past the island on the south side to land from the east. The airstrip is a narrow man made reef of hard sand fronting the marina requiring a dead stick landing. Cliff put her down easily and the Bahaman custom's official was already approaching in the standard mode of transport at Cat: the golf cart. We taxied back to the small white bus stop size custom check-in hut.

Cliff was going to have to wait for a Khalik as he had several passengers for his return to Florida. He got my bag, said to save him a spot at Boo's Bar for next time over, as he went on to meet and greet passengers. The Bahaman customs officer told me to wait by the hut while he made sure the out going crowd had their papers in order. After about ten unhurried minutes he motioned for me to hop on the cart, driving me around the marina to the white stone custom's house, tucked between several small stone cottages sporting fresh white paint and brightly colored doors. I filled out the custom form and paid my entry fees, always a reminder that the "residents" were foreign guests, a revocable privilege.

I walked down the small path to the marina. The concrete pathways were wide enough for two way golf cart traffic and I meandered past the Haigh House, a nineteenth century, three room stone cottage named after one of the original British officer island owners.   The Haigh House was next to the Boutique, stocked with over priced shirts and dresses logoed with a little cat perched on a key. The path turned right toward the deck of the restaurant that looked over the marina and then "Boo's Bar", a grass hut replica setting on the dock. My guess was it was named for good old "Boo", who either had endeared himself to the members of the Club with some outrageous conduct, or, the more likely scenario for Cat, he ponied up the cash himself, liking to drink under a cabana.

Five or six sailboats were docked at the marina, typically a stopover to Freeport, Atlantis, or the Caribbean. The middle docks had several seventy-five foot yachts and two beautiful white one hundred foot Hatteras. Alex's Merritt, Quiet Tidal, was docked along side a thirty-five foot Sundance. The Merritt, with tuna tower, slick lines and dramatic teak trim was the Harley Davidson in a line up of Gold Wings and Yamahas.

Walking down the dock, I saw the Captain, OB, down on all fours near the tuna door and ice well. He didn't see me so I casually leaned against the dock post and waited. OB wore light khaki shorts, Cabella tee shirt and A.B.E. insignia baseball cap. Nearing sixty, OB was still a rock, with strong arms, and hard but handsome, gentle face. Like most fishermen, he was rarely without sunglasses. Last time I saw OB he was on ESPN piloting Quiet Tidel for a deep sea fishing television special hosted by blue marlin painter Guy Harvey. OB had been in these waters most of his life and ESPN wanted the best.

As OB put the cover back on the ice well, he caught my shadow across the deck. Looking up he said: "Heard you were coming over today."

"Can I come aboard captain?" I said.

He motioned to come on to the deck: "Friend or foe?". His tone might have been whimsical but in light of the circumstances I wasn't sure.

"How's it going OB?" I said while shaking hands.

"It's going."

I knew not to expect much from OB. And I didn't want him to think that I wanted any information from him. He would tell me what he wanted me to know and when. So it surprised me when he said:

"Am I going to need your services Jake?"

With most people I would have turned the question back to them and asked if they thought they did. But with OB I said: "I don't think so."

"Hope you're right. The insurance investigator asked me if I had an attorney yet and I asked, what for? He said I should maybe think about it if they determined it was my fault the boat sunk. Whoever said the truth will set you free hasn't spent much time in the Bahamas."

"With your reputation OB, I wouldn't think you have much to worry about."

He smiled: "Jake, you and I forget our place sometimes. So do Alex and the rest of the Cat Cay fat cats. I know all the local boys, here and at Bimini, Walker, Cat Island, all the fishing ports. I can get you a boat slip or a tip on the wahoo or know who to call in a jam. But Nassau views Cat Cay as purely business. They'll let this little make believe colonial charade go on as long as their people are not being taken advantage of, but it's their island and their country and if they decide there is a point to be made, they are not afraid to make it. There are plenty of Bahamian Harvard and Yale grads and they are not to be underestimated or condescended to. The Caribbean is done. The next wave is in the Bahamas and they don't care if the Americans, British or the Arabs put the money down."

I said: "So why do they care about Alex's boat sinking? A boat sinking happens all the time here."

"If the insurance company or Merritt push the wrong people, they'll make it an issue. And I don't want caught in the crossfire. Alex is a good man, but captains can be replaced and the Bahamians can revoke captain licenses. And without a license for these waters...." He stopped. "That's enough of that."

OB turned away to open one of the fishing tackle compartments. OB was near the end of his captain days and he knew it. He was hoping to finish up with Alex. I said: "I'll be there if you need me OB, you know that."

He nodded. I said: "I'll be around a couple days I think. I

better head up to the house."

"Take the cart."

"I'll walk. Enjoy the weather. Maybe run into pretty Georgie."

I walked down the dock, past the restaurant and office, on past the small commissary to the open unguarded white wooden gates of the Cat Cay Club. Just before the entrance is a sign listing the "Club Members in Residence" announcing to other Cat "Key" holders who's "on island." Alex's name plate had been posted. I made my way down the paved path through the gate, palm trees on each side. None of the palms are indigenous to the island or the Bahamas. The palms were brought in from Florida as the residents like to think they're in Tahiti. Underneath one of the palms was Georgie, the local peacock, adding his color to paradise. Every neighborhood should have a peacock or two to go with their palms. Odd to no one on Cat, except the Bahamians.

Alex's "casa" sets on the opposite bay of the marina with a western vista. Beautiful sunsets, sailboats and dive boats anchored up as backdrop. Not a great place to be in a hurricane though, which average a monster every ten years. Hurricane aftermath recovery had become one of Dean's rituals, thus his constant push for Alex to sell his "Cat" house.

Walking around to the back I saw Alex through the glass sliding doors. He was talking on his cell phone. He waved me in with a big smile as I slid the door open and stood inside. He pointed to the fridge, with a simulated beer in hand, popping to his mouth, with a motion to "go ahead".

Through the living area to the small kitchen, I got a cold Khalik. Alex was standing at the glass looking out at the Atlantic, dressed in Bermuda shorts and Tommy Bahamas shirt. Alex was in the middle of his sixth decade, with a quarterback physique attributable to daily work outs, mainly swimming. His end of the conversation on the phone was:

"No. No. The guy sitting in the chair looking out the veranda with the girl gazing at him, that's Gustave Caillebotte. Renoir, The Boating Party. Caillebotte is the only one left out of that school remotely reasonable. Find the sketches. Where? I don't know. But I'm looking at a picture of the sketches right now!"

As I reentered the room, Khalik in hand, Alex walked over to me with cell in one hand and an open art book in the other, making me look at where he was pointing. Sure enough, it was a book on Caillebotte, open to pages on the sketches for his "Paris street" scene. Alex was no art collector, but he was a collector. Last time I was on Cat he was on a quest for originals of C. S. Forester's Hornblower series. When he found out Forester wrote African Queen, he started to collect Bogart memorabilia.

He continued. "Well, let me know. Miguel, sorry again about Jolene."

With that Alex hung up, put the art book down, walked over, and grabbed my right hand with a firm shake and an equally firm left hand on the forearm.

"Jake, good to see you. Can't stand the French, but god, would you not want to have lived in Paris in the 1890's? Did you ever meet Miguel?"

I said: "No."

"Good guy. Has a place here at Cat. Knew Castro." Alex said. "He's not really an art dealer. But he and I started collecting some paintings. Great market. Particularly with his Cuban connections. Miguel's wife's Jolene just died. Sweet women. Real classy lady. Chip saw her, and referred her to the best in New York, but there was nothing they could do."

Chip was Chip Leicht, a doctor with a general practice living in Nags Head now, but who often was the doctor of the week at Cat. He had become Alex's personal doctor. His own HMO.

"How was the flight? Cliff sober?"

I said: "This time."

He picked up his drink and said: "How are we making out with Mrs. Frampton?"

I started out answering him by bringing him up to date with my meetings with her and the Pittsburgh attorneys. In the middle of that Dave, his Bahamian yard man, peeked his head in the door. Alex said:

"What's up Dave?"

"Cap send me up. Said he need you about call. Said maybe important."

"Hey, Jake, do you mind? I better run down, been waiting for a call. Be right back. Make yourself at home. Come on Dave."

Home alone on a private island. I would try to make the best of it.

Chapter Six

—

I walked out to the patio and over to a telescope set on a tripod to view boats cruising and golden sunsets. Peering out I spied stacks with Mickey Mouse ears from the Big Red Boat out of Miami heading east with all those adorable brats. A tilt of the lens and a faded rusty "Angel" appeared. The words were all that was visible of the bow the Angelica, a cargo tanker that sunk six month ago off Cat. Just to the right of that was a dive boat. The Sanford and Sons of boats, with wetsuits hanging over rails, hibachi strapped aft, tanks roped to the rails, sails always half tied, dingy or two trailing behind, barking dog and no differentiation between crew and dive guests. Divers were a festive lot, ironic that their nature tours were focused on another man's misfortune. I had met the captain of the Angelica, who went down with the ship, and he seemed like a good guy.

Still perusing the dive boat, from behind me I heard: "Looking for sunbathers?"

Startled, but I recognized the voice heard only by phone over the last year. The last face to face with Trina ended with her saying: "I didn't ask you to fall in love with me. All I asked was for you to love me. Was that too much to ask?" I didn't answer because the question confused me.

Turning around, Trina was leaning against the open doorway dressed in a white terry cloth bathrobe brushing back her wet hair. She looked as she always did: imposingly gorgeous. A tall lithe woman, thick short jet black hair, light blue eyes, firm jaw, narrow mouth, tiny ears, and, let's say, demure nose. Body type that left you wondering if she worked out everyday, or was just naturally fit. Quick wit, great sense of humor, meaning she thought I was hilarious, and a compelling need for independence, unless she decided to be dependant for a day.

I put my Khalik down and I started toward her smiling. She leaned her hip to the door even more, still combing her showered hair. Getting a kick out of me not knowing what to do physically, she looked at me with a grin, or maybe it was a smirk. Approaching, avoiding body contact, worried about a stiff arm, I went for a light kiss. Trina turned her head slightly to the left, so I pecked her right cheek. She said: "This used to be British soil, aren't you going European?"

She turned her head back to the right and I gave her another slight peck on her left cheek. Settling that, she walked over to the telescope and looked out, saying:

"Like clock work, almost every other day, that dive boat from Bimini comes here to look over the bones of the crew of the Angelica." Moving the lens aside, she said: "So, what kind of trouble does father have the company in that his boy is down here at Cat?"

Right to business. "Boy" was a nice touch too. Alex's business structure was as complex as any over priced corporate business lawyer could bill. Limited liability companies under a family trust umbrella with a managing side corporation for day to day operations. Trina was the President of the corporation so technically I answered to her, but I wasn't sure if the sunken Merritt was paid for by one of the companies or Alex personally. Dangerous ground involving Trina's appearance of authority, as opposed to who actually ran the company.

"You tell me. You're the President." I said.

She stopped the combing and shot back: "Maybe before you get too involved you should remember that."

Getting to me quicker than I thought she would, I angrily said: "Come on. I don't need that bullshit. Whatever problems you have with dear old dad, leave me out of it."

No response, just a stare. I said: "Can't we start over?"

"Fuck you, Jake." She turned and walked back inside, sliding the door behind her.

It really was not *that* long a walk back down the path to the dock. Maybe I would have handled Trina better had I known in advance she was at Cat. Nice of Alex to tell me. She controlled whatever our relationship was two years ago, but would never admit it. She said I listened to the blues but never felt them because of the walls surrounding me. I remembered thinking that she just wanted to feel in love, and it didn't necessarily have to be me. We were both dime novel psychologists.

When I arrived at the dock, OB was washing down the boat. Alex not in sight, I asked: "Alex around?"

"He was. Got off the phone and said he was leaving on Velázquez's helicopter. Off he went."

Velázquez was the king of "coke" at Cat. Coca Cola that is, as he had the South American franchise for the last twenty years.

OB said: "Alex said to tell you that he would call you when he got a chance. Said to be nice to Trina." OB smiled at that.

"Hey. Thanks for telling me Trina was here." I said.

Grinning, he went back to hosing down the Quiet Tidal. I pulled out a Khalik from one of the teak built-in coolers that lined the back of the deck, beside the ice cooler. The main reason Alex spent millions on a new boat was that he didn't like the location of that cooler. I said: "What's up for tomorrow since I have no client, no purpose here?"

"I'm going over to Bimini if you want to go along. We heard a few marlin stories that I want to check out. Some of the locals are saying that they've seen a few off Bimini, and it would be a disaster if they're this close and Alex doesn't find them. Master Angler that he is."

Each year Alex participated in an elite fishing tournament, usually in Mexico or Venezuela, where the wealthy few with multimillion dollar Merritt's tried their luck finding sail fish. It was usually a question of who had the best captain, but that was not always a question of money.

I told OB I was in on the plan to Bimini. With Trina at the house, and me persona non gratis, the boat was now my abode. I put my bag in the guest cabin below. Back top side I moved a couple of folding chairs to the dock placing them about two feet apart facing the sun, which had about a half hour to set. OB was just putting away the hose so I grabbed a cloth, helped finish wiping down the sides, fetched two beers from the cooler and we sat down.

Coming here over forty years ago when Richard Nixon's

friend Bebe Robozo had a place, OB reminisced about what Cat Cay was like when he first started: "Cat has always been a rich man's island. More of a movie set than a culture. Bimini. A lot of changes there, even from when you were there three or four years ago. You'll see for yourself tomorrow."

Wanting to ask about the sinking of the Merritt, but figuring there was a better time, OB surprised me saying: "I'll tell you one thing that has changed around here and that's the dwindling number of ladies and gentlemen on board since Mrs. Beckett stopped coming over."

Mrs. Beckett was Alex's wife, whom he divorced some time ago. He continued, back tracking slightly: "Don't get me wrong, the people we have on board are very nice, mostly respectful, but not that same. How do I put it Jake?"

"The difference between Lauren Becall and Demi Moore. Humphrey Bogart and Brad Pitt."

"Yeah." He raised his glass to me and said: "Here's looking at the old days, kid."

I nodded: "Which category did George Frampton fit into?"

He took a long sip, sat back, just catching the sun going down and said: "You know, odd as it sounds, I never met him."

"But he was on the boat when it sank."

"That's what they tell me. Mike Clontz brought Frampton's gear on board. I helped stow it. Mike told me Frampton was below working on his laptop. As soon as we got out of the dock area, Mike came up on top to the tower where I was steering, checking out controls and said Frampton needed some sea sick pills. I told Mike to get him to the deck, figuring once we got out further we could open it up more and kill the rocking. That usually cures it."

He looked over at me with an eye for reminding me of my last fishing trip with OB and Trina where I spent the first day hung over the side.

"OB, believe me, I'm not here to interrogate you, but what happened to him?"

"I don't know. When Mike finally went below, all hell broke loose."

Not sure if OB was going to offer any more, I didn't press. I did ask if Mike Clontz was around, thinking of talking to him the next day. OB told me he hadn't seen him since the accident. His tone told me Clontz was not high on OB's respect list, but that's what you get with the transient mates. We sat there maybe another half hour not really talking about anything in particular when the Bahamian waiter, Leland, from Boo's Bar appeared dressed in black pants, white shirt, bow tie, gold vest. He had in his hand a tray, with a single drink in the middle.

Saying good evening to OB, he looked at me, lowering the tray: "Miss Trina send d'is over. Captain Coke."

Taking the drink as if booby trapped, saying thanks, I handed Leland a five. I turned my head as Leland walked back to Boo's Bar, seeing a lady sitting, assuming it was Trina.

I said to OB: "You wouldn't mind testing this for me, would you?"

OB rose, folded up his chair, grinned, and walked away saying: "Be strong my son."

I sat a few minutes, sipping the drink, and then submissively made my way over to my second meeting of the day with Trina. I was feeling an old weakness coming on strong.

Chapter Seven

———

Trina was sitting at the bar facing the docks playing with a cigarette. I picked the stool to the left to sit on and before I could thank her for the drink, she said, pointedly: "No comment on the cigarette."

Actually I took the nicotine fix as a good sign as she only smoked when in a tawdry mood. She motioned for Leland to bring us another drink, hers a Korbel. She said:

"Leland and I were just discussing Kirkland's lack of understanding of men. Weren't we Leland?"

Leland glanced over with a look that suggested *he* was not discussing much of anything. Kirkland was Leland's girl friend on Cat, seen together mostly at low tide between Cat and South Cat searching for conch. Leland decided he fortuitously needed more ice. He smiled and headed to the restaurant, leaving me alone with Trina.

"Do you know anything about Charles Darwin and natural selection, professor?" She asked.

"A little." I said.

She said, the way a drinking woman draws out a phrase: "A little. Well. Here's what I was telling our bartender. To help him out with Kirkland."

"That's benevolent of you." I said with a hint of sarcasm.

Ignoring that, she went on: "You guys are genetically programmed to have sex all the time. Can't help it. If honesty works, that's good. Buying it, that can be good. Deception, if necessary. Do you not agree, Mr. Quinn?"

"Probably."

"Good. See. We're already off to a better start."

She offered her glass to tip to, to which I complied. She continued: "Now men seek the prettiest and healthiest women they can catch with what they got. Not that they really think about it. It's a sheer numbers game for your gender, wanting to get as many of your little guys out there as possible. The obsession is the sex. You're carrying an unlimited supply of ammunition. You can't help it, right, firing all the time?"

"I suppose."

"Right. Natural selection is the engine, but the by-product is fitness."

She paused. I just nodded, wondering where this was going. She continued:

"What about me? Women, we're different. A limited supply of eggs. Maybe no more than three hundred in a lifetime. She has to be careful. She can't just be out there handing them out. She needs to protect her supply and more importantly the resulting baby. Someone to protect her. Her genes are telling her the handsomest and strongest are best suited to accomplish the task. Her quest is set. Not a lot she can do about it."

"Ok." I said, deciding to join in, which I knew was a mistake: "So what about the young woman who goes after the older man. How does that fit?"

"No different than any other puppet of natural selection. She can't help herself. She's looking for the best male and what better than one with a proven track record. The fact he already has a mate and kids is just proof he is worthy and has some fine genes. That makes the attraction even greater."

She seemed about to conclude that topic pleased with her thoughts, when she said looking out over the marina:

"Hell, society rewards the older male as long as he pays for the one he left. Legal polygamy. Why not? You guys still control the world cultures."

She took a drag on her cigarette as I said, slyly: "What about men pursuing beautiful wealthy women."

"You left out older."

"Did I?" I said.

"Since you asked. Men have inherent problems with successful women. The male resists an independent mate. Some can handle it, some can't."

Squaring her face to mine, moving closer, past my left cheek, she whispered, not sultry, not secretively, but quietly:

"That's why you don't understand your feelings about me. A consciousness that I'm not, and never will be, dependent on you is a challenge. It defies your natural selection forces. And it keeps you from loving me."

She moved back and picked up her cigarette. I knew then that there was much less alcohol in Trina than I led myself to believe and that this was not an unrehearsed anthropology lecture.

I said: "Does my reaction determine if we have sex tonight?"

Answering without hesitation: "We're having sex tonight, buddy, no matter what your answer. After that, answers and natural selection matter."

Leland had just returned and I said: "Leland, I definitely need another drink."

"Sure d'ing."

I said to Trina: "I don't know about all that. I will admit this: it has been a mistake to be away from you for so long. But here I am for whatever reason now." I paused and then said: "The rest of the evening is up to you."

Leland put my drink in front of me just as I finished speaking. Trina put a fifty down, picked up her drink and her purse, and smiled at Leland, then asking me:

"Take a walk?"

We walked past the front of the restaurant toward the boats and pier feeling the late night cool Bahaman breeze, hearing the rhythms and beat from the distant Haigh House and gentle sounds of Bob Marley. Approaching the end of the pier Trina gingerly stopped ahead of me, turned with a dip, came back up facing me, and slowly raised her hands above her head and started to dance, seductively, catching Marley's tune:

"One love...."

She crossed her arms in front of her, swaying to the beat.

"One heart..."

She pointed to her heart with a cat like smile.

"Let's get together and feel alright..."

Shuffling toward me, pointing at herself then me, then herself, then me, then took my arms and put them on her shoulders, and slowly brought her face to mine, tapped her forehead against mine, rubbed her slightly red nose lightly against mine, and mouthed. *"Let's get together and feel alright..."* She moved back just a bit and said:

"Night cap, Haigh House, my house?"

Taking her hand, we headed back down the pier, walking past the Pharaoh, the seventy-five foot wooden hulled cruiser owned by Kamal Fasal, a naturalized American by way of Cairo. Kamal started worldwide travel about a decade ago with his dazzling wife Natasha. With Kamal being vertically challenged and his pencil mustache, they were the reality version of Boris and Natasha of Bullwinkle cartoon fame.

Kamal was a civil engineer who had worked his way around the world and corporate headquarters finally settling in Pittsburgh. I did not meet Kamal originally on Cat, but at a farm he owned near my office in Amish country. Kamal's hobby was painting in his studio on the farm, where he produced Gougan like large breasted dark skinned endomorph natives. The walls being adorned with these original works of bare breasted ladies, Kamil's house had become a gathering place for the young and old local Amish men.

Natasha was Slovakian, Kamal having met her in England via Prague from where her family fled from in the late 1930's to escape Hitler's Arian madness. Natasha, now in her 60's, was tall, still slender, pitch black long hair, a handsome pure high cheeked face, and a European lady chic. She was charming and gracious. As a couple they showed none of the combativeness and resignation so often found in aging duos. Ten years ago, with Alex's input, Kamal sold his engineering company and bought the Pharaoh shortly thereafter. Cat Cay became a regular winter retreat along with trips to Nassau, Freeport, and on to the Caribbean.

Pharaoh's lights were on as we walked by and we heard Kamal's distinctive Arabic accent:

"Jake! Trina!" Then less loud: "Natash. Get the Glenfiddich! Trina and Jake are here."

Kamal was quickly off his deck and on to the pier with a bear hug for Trina and outstretched double hand shake for me.

Shortly we were inside on the screened upper deck, exchanging kisses with Natasha and sipping a cold single malt scotch. Trina and Natasha caught up on their kids as Kamal and I talked about Pharaoh's various destinations over the last several months. A half hour into this boating party, the conversation turned to events on Cat, with Kamal inquiring of Trina:

"I was sorry to hear of your father's boat being lost, the locals say they have not found it yet."

Trina said: "Not yet. We think it went down in pretty deep water."

"Kamil, I understand the first mate was from your boat." I said.

Natasha glanced at Kamil. A wife's protective glance for the husband to be careful what he was about to say or reveal. He said: "Was. Our captain let him go after that. He's back in Miami."

Natasha, looking at Trina, added: "I did not like being alone with him. Constantly taking off his shirt so we could see his Neptune navy submarine tattoo."

Trina nodded approval to the women's unspoken universal power that they can feel such things.

Kamal said: "Elizabeth Frampton didn't share those feelings, my dear."

Kamal got "the look" from Natasha on that one. Diverting attention from his possibly unwise revelation, he said to me: "One more."

Glancing at Trina, I did not get approval, and I hoped I was reading her correctly that one more drink could jeopardize her plans for me later. I said:

"Kamal, old friend. Natasha. We have a full day tomorrow and I promised Trina's daddy that I would not keep her out past midnight."

We exchanged good-byes discussing a get together state side in the fall. Trina and I restarted our walk back to Alex's taking us past the Haigh House, where the loud Jamaican music was still pounding. The Haigh House was now a community center, so to speak, where the Bahamans who worked on Cat during the week drank, listened to music, and watched American sports on television, principally NBA basketball. Premium marijuana could be had for the asking. Another time, I might have stopped in, had a drink, bought a round, and played some pool, but I was thinking we both had other thoughts so we continued past, easing down the lane, sounds of chickens, peacocks, and the Haigh House fading.

Walking around to the ocean facing patio, we could hear the waves slapping on the shore. Lights on, doors never locked. Inside, Trina proceeded to the laundry closet around the corner near her bedroom, and returned with a washcloth, towel, and robe, pitching them all in my direction while pointing to the guest shower. She turned and walked toward her bedroom removing her top over her head showing her strong back and a turquoise bra, being unsnapped as she closed the door behind her. I eagerly pulled a Khalik out the fridge on my way to the shower.

I quickly showered, threw on the robe and made my way into the living room, lighted now with candles. On the couch listening to the soft sound of the waves through the open windows, I heard Trina behind me as she put her hands on the back of the couch, swinging her hips and legs over, landing on her butt with her feet on my lap. She was dressed in a silk blue top, with her hair still slightly wet. No socks.

"Foot rub?" She said.

I snatched her feet, went about my assignment, making gentle massages and rubs on her right foot, then the arches, then each manicured toe, pushing the trapped and confused energy out the tips, repeating the whole process on the left foot minutes later. All the while Trina was making diminutive sounds, sinking further and further into the couch. As I started back on the right foot again, Trina looked up and said:

"You know the real reason I left Dean?"

"No." I said, which she ignored, proceeding to say: "Not because he was a lousy lover, which he was. Not because he was a lousy dad, which he was. But because he just didn't get it when it came to foot rubs. He had the mechanics, but no passion."

She pulled her feet and knees to her chest, hugged them a

few seconds, and then rotated around, putting her feet on the floor and slightly tilting her head to me, with a kind of whisper smile. She held out her hand to me, I rose slowly and she walked me to her bedroom.

Leading me to the side of the bed sensing perhaps my nervousness, she patted it for me to sit down, which I did. She moved and stood between my knees hanging over the edge of the bed. Grabbing my knees, she pressed them against her thighs, wiggling slightly to adjust to just the right fit. She put her arms around the back of my neck and whispered: "I missed you."

She turned her head slightly, gently putting her lips against mine and we kissed for the first time in more than two years. A motionless unreasoned unpressured embrace, more than enough to bridge, for now, the gap time had created. I don't know how long we kissed before it led to hugs and slight tugs, but I was the gentle lead in a sensual waltz performed by long ago lovers who had danced that same dance before. Not whimsical, not aggressive, although the temptation in either direction was palpable. The release and relief, as much satisfying as necessary, overwhelming and calming. Lost in the wave.

As she snuggled against my side, me gently stroking her hair, she hummed or mumbled something softly as she drifted off to sleep. I thought she was saying softly: "Sending me angels, just like you....."

Chapter Eight

U p at dawn, I quietly placed a morning cup of java on Trina's nightstand as she slept. I went for a run on the concrete paths of the Windsor Downs's nine hole course through the middle of Cat. When I returned and showered, Trina had prepared a breakfast set on the patio table. Eating and talking about the evening in pleasant tones, I told her about plans of going over to Bimini with OB to ask around about the missing Merritt. She informed me, as if at a corporate meeting, that she had already talked to OB and *we* were leaving in a half hour. It was a metaphor for our previous relationship: me slipping back into my role as hired hand. She maybe was right about me not coming to terms with her independence. Or worse, her being in a superior position. But it was her dime, her boat. Half hour later we were with OB on the *Quiet Tidal*, untying the slip ropes, making our way to Bimini.

Ten miles northeast of Cat Cay, Bimini was Papa Hemmingway's island. Famous for *Islands in the Stream, Old Man and the Sea,* and where he wrote *To Have and to Have Not.* Hemmingway reigned during the 1930's, staying at the Compleat Angler Hotel, a museum shrine to him now with Key Largo thirties atmosphere, wooden bar area, and original fading photos of Papa. In the fifties and sixties big game fishing was still king and so was native and 1960's Congressman, Adam Clayton Powell. But Hemmingway, Powell and the big game fish are gone. Now it's wahoo, bottom fishing, and scuba diving, all over shadowed by drug running.

OB had us at Bimini in an hour making his usual effortless slide up to the dock at the Big Game Fishing Club, proper flags flying on the rail denoting we had already passed customs at Cat. Trina and I jumped to the dock and tied up. OB locked down

Quiet Tidal, put on the alarm and the three of us started a trek through Bimini. Past the Howard Johnson looking Big Game Club, we walked by "The Compleat Angler", noting no customers, same as my last trip over. We needed to go past the "Angler" to get to the scuba shop, our destination, but as OB knows most of the captains and mates on the islands, it did not take long before he was in a conversation, motioning for us to go ahead. OB said he was coming over to find out about the marlin, but he told me he was as interested as I was in any scuttlebutt about the sunken Merritt.

Trina and I went ahead noting the same junk and messy streets as on all the islands in the Caribbean and Bahamas. Not filth as much as "stylish abandonment" on all the side streets. Walking past locals sitting on the doorsteps, I felt slightly susceptible to some Bimini trouble, as opposed to Trina who moved ahead as if she owned the place. A couple minutes later we were at the scuba shop which was in a squared off two story cement block building with a balcony that looked over the entrance to the bay. We advanced up the outside stairs to the scuba shop door, checking the literature in the outside case describing countless dive opportunities with scantly attired young ladies.

Trina proceeded inside, me following. Behind the counter on a stool was a petite attractive Bahamian in her early twenties, braided hair and long red nails. She was glancing at the counter television showing the Home Shopping Channel out of Miami while at the same time she worked on a notebook computer. She acknowledged our presence with a pleasant smile saying: "May I help you?"

Trina answered quizzically: "Vicki?"

Excitedly she said: "Oh, Mrs. McDonald." She quickly came around the counter and they exchanged hugs. "McDonald" threw me off as Trina had long since changed her name back to Beckett.

Trina's apparent old but young acquaintance said: "Are Scott and Todd with you?"

"No. Just me, the boys are in college. You sure have grown up. Last time I talked to your dad he said you were finishing up your MBA at Miami."

"Yeah. I graduate next month. Uncle Don wanted me to help him out here for a week. He owns the building. I'm trying to put in an accounting system. He asked me to watch the building this morning, and then the scuba shop guys were short handed, so here I am. What are you doing over here?"

"We came over with OB. He's checking out rumors of a marlin run." Pointing to me: "We brought along our mouth piece, Jake Quinn." We exchanged greetings, both thinking we might have met before on a previous trip. Trina said: "I wanted to talk to the guys' scuba diving off our doorstep at Cat. Do you know who's running the dive shop now?"

"I can pull up the accounting records and see what that says, but I can tell you they're a little spooky."

"How's that?" I interjected.

She explained her comment while searching on her computer: "They never seem to accept any bookings, but are always out diving. And the dive crews are all good looking big Yankees, different every week. What do you call them, the ones that are all military?"

"Seals?" I answered.

"I don't know for sure. Like the ROTC guys at Miami U. Or maybe your Coast Guard. Polite. But cocky and all business. Uncle Don doesn't complain, he gets his check like clock work."

She paused, hitting more keys, then said: "Here we go. Tad Industries foots the bill."

Trina asked: "Does it give an address?"

"Not really. The money's wired into Uncle Don's bank account from Tad Industries bank."

I said: "Vicki, have you heard anything about the Merritt from Cat Cay that sank?"

"Not much. Other than some locals are trying to locate it for salvage. They've been going out at night looking for it. I don't leave the shop much anymore. I'm leaving next week. It's not really safe here anymore at night. Too much drugs, too little to do. The drugs used to just make them stupid and lazy. Now it makes them stupid and violent."

Trina and Vicki talked some more about Trina's sons and

getting together. After a few minutes we thanked her and left, heading past the gauntlet, deflecting wary looks, meeting up with OB coming out of the Compleat Angler. Trina mentioned wanting to stop at the local lunch shop for conch chowder. OB, to my surprise, pulled captain rank and said no. We had to get back, now. OB's pace was hurried and without conversation. At the boat, firm cast away instructions were given by OB and we were churning through the shallow Atlantic quickly.

OB relaxed the further Bimini faded from sight. Trina picked up a paperback she had started on the way over and dropped down to the lower deck. OB and I stayed up on top. When OB was sure Trina was out of ear shot he related to me observations and conversations on Bimini. Bimini was in a rapid rate of decline but still had some good people calling it home. One was Papa John, an old respected flat boat guide who was also the local minister. Papa could save your marriage, find you a job or get you out of jail. Off island work permits were punched by Papa.

OB said Papa was surprised we came over. The government, either Bahamian or the United States, was increasing drug interdiction and local dealers were temporarily out of work, waiting this cycle out, getting bored and high and drunk. Papa said the drug dealers were very interested in the sunken Merritt and recommended we leave Bimini quickly. With Trina under his watch he decided not to take any chances. Papa said he would be in touch as he owed Alex many favors. Naturally.

OB was cranking Quiet Title more than usual and in the shallow water off Bimini was glued to the radar so I went below to check my email. In a small office area off the stateroom below, Alex had equipped the Quiet Tidal with latest technology, including internet via the satellite. Passing Trina on the way below she invited me to sit, patting the seat beside her. I said I would be right back.

Once below I logged on to my email. Eva had a few updates from the office, not needing a response. Christine Napore, emailing from London, said she would be back in the states in two weeks and was I still single? Christine was a contract and labor lawyer for H. J. Heinz Corporation and we entertained each other on occasion. She said I kept her amused while she waited for the love lottery to call her number. I deferred on a response, for now.

My last message was from Bryan:

From: Bryan@Techtives.net
To: JQLaw@adelphia.net

Have some information on your deceased topic, Mr. Frampton. He is showing up in quite a few places. I put together some print articles we can look at when you get back. This guy was into some interesting stuff. Nicole says hi.

I typed a quick acknowledgment, thanking Bryan, letting him know I would be in touch. Deleting my messages, I logging off, while glancing at a printed email lying beside the printer. Seeing the name at the top, I read it:

From: Honorable Richard Taupin@USCongress.com
To: TrinaD@ABEnt.com

Trina: Call me. Dick

Richard Taupin was the fourth term United States Congressman from my district. Taupin was in his forties, handsome, charming and recently divorced. He was a career politician whose star was rising. He remained on a short list for Pennsylvania's next Senate opening. It helped that his freshman congressional class friend was ex-governor Tom Ridge, Homeland Security head. He had the skills of a good politician: listening, letting the public shape his thoughts and then saying what they wanted him to hear. I respected his ability to have no original thoughts. Long termers like Taupin learn that to stay in office they can't display to the public the power they truly wield. The eighth habit of highly effective politicians is to handle matters behind closed doors. But my reservations about Taupin weren't his career, they were more personal. When Trina and I

38

were "an item", she chaired several fund raisers for Taupin. It seemed to me she was always taking inopportune calls from his staff, with him eventually getting on the line.

As I walked past Trina she was still reading, and she glanced up and said: "I thought you were joining me. Trouble with Eva at the office?"

"No." And without thinking, heard myself say: "How are you and Congressman Taupin these days?"

She put her book down slowly: "What brought that on? As if it is any of your business."

"He wants you to call him."

The dark stare back. "You shouldn't read other people's email."

"You shouldn't intentionally put yours on display. But, hey, it's none of my business."

She answered abruptly: "I didn't, Ob must have printed it and you're right, it's none of your business."

I put my hands up: "I am just passing through. Don't mind me." I started to move on, when she said:

"I don't owe you an explanation about Taupin or anyone else. Is it jealousy, Jake? It's back to the same old thing, isn't it?"

"What's that?" I responded harshly.

"You like the idea of being with a real woman, except when you have to see her acting like one."

Becoming mantra, I said: "What does that mean?"

"It means this. How much company business that you get from my father do you think has to do with your actual skills? You guys golf, fish, hunt, drink, and talk about women and sports. He likes you. God only knows why? Men feel good being around a guy's guy like you. You do business together. Right so far?"

"Sure. But…"

She cut me off: "Do you think guys like to be around pretty women?"

"Given." I affirmed.

"So, of course, with your open mind, you think attractive women can use that. The guy feels good being around women like that. Kind of a guy's woman. They conduct business together. Are we still on the same page Jake?"

I nodded, realizing I was already well along the road of one of Trina's question and answer drills.

She continued, more assertive: "But with all us smart people knowing these games, I don't grow weary of making sure I'm never alone with a male friend or acquaintance at meetings. Nor do I get weary having to smile at the off-color humor, the childish porn pictures, or even the isolation and hostility of less independent women. It's part of business. The ante for playing the game. You know, I don't even grow weary of men and women thinking that if you have a male friend that you've got to be sleeping with him. You know what makes me weary though?"

I tried to sound earnest in my answer saying simply: "No, what?"

She looked at me, not with intense, but reflective eyes: "When a man who I thought I respected and who I thought respected me, can't comprehend what I just said. The self delusion of you and my father, thinking they can have a relationship with an independent woman."

I said defiantly: "I'm not jealous or afraid of your independence."

Trina snapped back: "If you can't lie any better than that, you might as well tell the truth Jake."

She snatched her book and walked past me. I stood there awhile knowing that we were really too close to the core problem of why we no longer saw each other. Yeah, I understood everything she said. I was, for Christ's sake, not an idiot. I just wanted to know: Was she goddamn sleeping with him or not? Was that too much to ask?

Chapter Nine

—

Sitting on the coolers, staring at the wash from the propellers, any top side noise drowned out by the twin diesels, Bimini was becoming a dot on the horizon. Trina had gone to the bridge to better ignore me and sit with OB when I noticed two small boats coming out of Bimini. We were taking a less direct route back to Cat Cay past the concrete World War II boat that was sunk by the Navy in the shallows. The boats out of Bimini were now headed toward us and coming fast. I hopped down from the coolers, climbed part way up the aluminum ladder to the bridge and yelled up to OB:

"Are you expecting company today?"

"No, if you mean the two boats following us. I've been watching them too. They look like pencil boats out of Bimini. Sometimes they stop at Cat to fuel up. They can out run anything the Bahaman police or the Coast Guard have. Drug runner's favorite."

"Well, they seem to be heading our way, not to Cat."

He said quietly: "I know. Go below and get the guns. I'm going to open it up more, but if they're after us, they'll catch us before we get to Cat."

I turned, went back down the ladder, into the cabin, down the steps to the crew quarters and opened the floor hatch to the engine room. Descending into the engine room, I opened a large tool cabinet mounted to the hull and found the disguised latch inside that swung the whole cabinet aside. It was easy to hide weapons there and the Coast Guard wouldn't tear your boat apart to find them. I found the silver aluminum case and brought it up to the main cabin. The case held a disassembled shotgun, a flair gun, a 50 caliber revolver hand gun, and a couple boxes of ammunition. Assembling and loading the shotgun and the 50 caliber, I put a handful of rounds in my right pocket, loaded the flair gun and stuck that in my belt with an extra flair round in my other pocket. As I got back on deck, the Quiet Tidal roared forward throwing me on to the deck almost over the side. OB had both diesels at full throttle. As I started to move to the ladder to go up to OB he screamed: "Get down!" At the same time, the cabin glass shattered, as bullets traced across the teak decking. OB yelled again: "Get down! Get down!"

OB was fully exposed, as was Trina, although she was trying to get behind the protection of the control panel. OB was crouched on his knees with hand on the wheel now starting to cut long zig zags across the flat ocean to make a larger wake area. He knew it would be harder for them to get off a straight shot with their light boats bouncing across the wake. But that wouldn't be much help when they were close. I jumped off the ladder and hunkered down below the sides. I could see now that there was a driver and passenger in each boat approaching on either side. The passenger's each had weapons pointing at us.

OB yelled down to me: "Throw me the shotgun."

Throwing the shotgun up, OB stood briefly to grab it as more bullets raked the deck and the area around OB and Trina. I heard OB scream: "Shit." Seconds later Trina yelled: "OB's been hit."

"Where?" I said.

"I don't know. His arm and leg I think."

I could just see Trina dragging OB back behind the control panel. The Quiet Tidal was unpiloted, making a long meandering turn. Our pursuers were within a few hundred feet, firing randomly. I yelled for Trina to get ready to take over the controls. Trina said, in an alarmed but not a panicked voice: "What are we going to do?"

"Just be ready to take the controls when I say."

Taking out the flair gun, I pointed it to the back of the deck and fired. There was a delay after the flair hit and exploded with smoke pouring over the deck area. Reloading I fired again at the same spot. Both flairs created a large black cloud which was engulfing our boat. I could see the pencils barely through the haze and dark smoke. Trina had the shotgun in her hands. The cork plug had been removed from the twelve gauge shotgun and I had loaded six magnum rounds. I yelled: "Cut the throttle and fire at the one on the right."

She cut the engine and the Quiet Tidal went dead in the water, the pursuers now less than twenty yards behind. I heard the shotgun blasts from above as I rose to fire the 50 caliber handgun at the boat on the left. The noise was horrific, the kick almost tearing the gun out of my hand as the barrel flashed from the fire port. If the bullet hit anyone he would be dead instantly and if I missed it would still tear through the fiberglass boat's hull. I fired all six rounds as did Trina. Neither of us could see what impact we made. I yelled to Trina:

"Full throttle. Full throttle."

The Quiet Tidal's twins roared as Trina pushed both throttle arms down. We emerged from the flair smoke seeing that Trina had put several rounds into the front of the pencil she was firing at. It was dead in the water. But the boat I was firing at was not out of commission, smoke trailing from its engine area, still coming on, and veering back and forth. The passenger had a rifle in hand and continued firing at random. I climbed up the ladder handing Trina more shotgun shells, telling her to reload. I took over the wheel pushing her to the front of the boat. As she crawled forward, I decided to spin the Quiet Tidal. I slowed the throttle, spun the wheel a hard left, as I did Trina was thrown into the side of the boat, the shotgun flew from her hand into the water. The pencil boat veered to the right, but the wake caught just enough of its front end to slow it down. I pushed both throttles down and our bow slammed into it. I looked back seeing the engine compartment ripped open, the driver scrambling out of his seat. I kept the throttles open and started making a wide turn toward Cat Cay.

Trina was up and checking on OB, who was conscious, but in shock. She went below to get the first aide kit and a shirt for a tourniquet. I kept checking back to see if we were being pursued as Trina dressed OB's wounds. I put Quiet Tidal on auto pilot and checked the boat. Plenty of damage, with most of the windows shot out and numerous holes, but all above the sea line.

An hour later we limped into the Cat Cay harbor and

stretchered OB to the doctor's office. Trina asked me who I thought did it and I said either government pressure was cracking the drug runners who now were taking random chances in open daylight, or, the more personal scenario: someone wanted us to join George Frampton at the bottom of the Bahamian waters.

Chapter Ten

Trina and I stayed on at Cat Cay the night of the attack, having spent some of the day answering the Bahamian customs officer's questions. No one seemed in too big a hurry to race over to Bimini since there was little chance of finding the shooters. The pencil boats were now either at the bottom, or hidden somewhere on or near Bimini. Everyone knows everyone else's business on the islands, but that doesn't mean they talk to the police. Before I left I asked around about George Frampton with some locals at the Cat Cay office, learning no more than I already didn't know.

We flew back state side the following afternoon. I arranged to catch a flight north and Trina had business of her own in Florida. We didn't talk much, keeping our thoughts to ourselves. OB was at the Fort Lauderdale General Hospital and Trina dropped me off there saying she would be checking on him later. It was an uneventful sterile departure for both of us.

OB was still in intensive care, suffering a bullet wound to his right arm, right leg, and fragment in this lung. I spoke briefly to the nurse who said I could see him for a few minutes. OB was in a glass enclosed bedside area, barely awake, numerous IV's and monitoring devices attached. I went to his side and said:

"They say they can't keep an old sea dog down. How you doing Captain?"

OB said, groggily: "OK, thanks to you and Trina. I owe you one Jake."

"Well, we owe someone a payback. Any ideas?"

Grimacing, he turned toward me, moving an IV, and saying: "No. Not really."

Maybe I was sensing things not there, but he was holding back. I said: "You sure. I don't want to be left out."

45

"Isn't that what Crockett said at the Alamo to Travis and Boone." OB said with a weak smile.

"Drug runners?"

He avoided the question and said intensely, as if visualizing and predicting the future: "As soon as I get out of here, I'll find out. And that will be the end of it."

The nurse came back in and told me I had to go. I told OB Trina would be in to check on him. He thanked me again and I left thinking OB meant to find who did it and probably had more resources than anyone to do just that. In his condition it was going to be awhile so the revenge would be served cold.

I caught a cab to Alex's house located on one of the many canals that maze through Lighthouse Point leading to the Intercostals then the Atlantic. Although the lots were small, the locations were premiere with dock access out the patio door. New buyers typically paid millions, then tore down the existing house and rebuilt. One block away, off the channel, a similar house sold for a fraction.

Dami, Alex's fifties petit motherly Cuban maid, cook, part time secretary answered the door, greeting me with a warm hug. Dami was another Alex story. I had mentioned to Alex one day while fishing near Cuban waters that one of our law school professors was Cuban and had actually served with Fidel Castro, but had escaped. When the professor came to the states he had left most of his family behind who never got out. I said that I had gotten word from a classmate that the professor was very ill. The story intrigued Alex. He arranged unofficially through the Canadian Consulate to find Dami and have her see her father before he died. She and her family never returned to Cuba and all ended up working for Alex. The loyalty was to the core. I never mentioned anything to Dami, but I think she knew I might have had some connection.

Dami and I talked about her kids as she directed me to Alex in his office, which was a large open room, more a patio that had a view of the intercostals. Alex, as usual on the phone, greeted me by a wave and pointed to a rattan chair. Just as I sat down, to my left, came a soft British voice:

"Mr. Quinn. So nice to see you again. Alex said you would

be dropping by. Can I offer you a beverage?"

She was dressed strikingly different than the last time we met in Corning. A flowered wrap around skirt, with a lycra top that clung tightly to her expensive chest. No shoes, her blonde hair back with a small flower off her ear. Great shoulders, with a commandingly coy smile. Mrs. Frampton had star billing as Alex's sophisticated Floridian companion.

I said: "Well, I can't stay long, but whatever you're having is fine with me."

"Actually," she said glancing a quick smile at Alex, "I just mixed a fruit cocktail. I'll get us both one."

She left, turning toward the entrance to the kitchen area, at about the time Alex was hanging up the phone. As she walked to go back to the bar area just inside, I caught Dami eyeballing Alex's new "lady friend", sensing no love lost between these women. Dami had seen an assortment of "flowered companions" over the years and none had made it into her tribe yet.

Alex hung up and said: "What? Is she getting you her fruit cocktail? I swear to god, everyday she tries some new combination. Perhaps they don't have fruit in England. I have to admit, one out of two isn't bad."

He walked over to the chair beside me, sat down and continued, seeming to want to speak quickly before his housemate came back.

"Wow, sorry I wasn't there to help out. I hear OB was hurt pretty bad, but is doing ok. Any information on who did it?"

I said without expression: "No, we're thinking drug runners. At least that's what the Bahamian's think. They've got some people working on it but I don't expect much."

"Where's Trina?"

"She dropped me off at the hospital. I think she plans on going over to see OB later, after that I don't know. I've got a flight in a couple hours."

I decided it was a good time to ask his lady friend a few questions so I said:

"Alex, I did not know Mrs. Frampton was here, but since she is, do you mind if I ask her some questions?"

Alex's response was quick and level: "Be my guest."

Elizabeth Frampton walked in with our drinks Alex saying: "Jake needs some of your time about your case."

"Sure." She said as she sat down across from me, legs on display, placing the tray of drinks on the small table. She handed me my drink with a napkin, took a sip of hers, placing it properly back on the table, leaning back, casually, not provocatively, but not giving up any of her feminine advantage.

I said: "I've been trying to pin down, even though I'm not sure if it makes any difference, who your husband had contact with at Cat the day before the accident. Did you see him that day?"

"You mean the day of the accident or the day before."

"Either."

Without hesitation, she said: "Well, if I remember right, we flew over a couple days before to join Alex. I think Alex was with us. George was interested in going over to Sandy Cay."

She turned to Alex: "Dear, do you recall when George came over to Cat."

"I don't. But I think I was already there.".

She looked back at me and said: "Well, there you go, I guess I don't remember."

I said: "I stopped at Island Air yesterday, and checked the manifest and it only shows you and Alex going over two days before."

She never took her eyes off me and shrugged: "Gee, maybe he flew over earlier or came over with OB on the Quiet Tidal."

"I checked all the flights, he's listed the day before you and Alex, but the pilot couldn't remember one way or the other."

She said sharply, this time glancing at Alex, getting no backup as he was now on his cell phone: "Does it make any difference how he got over?"

"I guess not, I'm just trying to figure out who he had contact with before he died."

I decided not to let it go just yet. "Gail at the Cat's management office talked to Cat customs and they have him on the island the day before with a custom sign in form, but she says he hadn't checked plane or boat as to how he got there, and customs must have just missed it. Do you have his passport?"

"No. I assume it went to the bottom with the boat."

"Did you talk to him before he left?"

"Just briefly. Like I said, he was hoping they were going past Sandy Cay. He wanted to check out the sand operation there."

I changed gears. "I don't know anything about your husband."

She liked the change of topic as she was obviously uncomfortable with trying to explain why no one saw her husband before he died. She said: "What do you want to know?"

She reached into her purse, pulled out a cigarette and lit it, all the while starring directly at me. Alex, still on the phone, frowned seeing the cigarette.

I said: "How about something simple, like: what did your husband do for a living?"

She took a sophisticated drag, let it out slowly, and said contemplatively: "Do you like my drink?"

I took a drink. Too fruity for me, but it was good. "It's cute."

She said with posed contemptuousness: "George? How would I describe what George did for a living? Let me see. He liked to consider himself a consultant. Alex probably has one of his cards in his office somewhere. If I remember it says: George Frampton, *Silicon Medium Consultant.*"

I said: "How long were you married?"

"I married George three years ago. We met when he was lecturing in England. If Alex didn't tell you, I was a flight attendant for British Airways. George flew over quite often and we hit it off. He was quirky but nice. Honestly, Mr. Quinn, our relationship was not great over the last year." She seemed to be directing that statement toward Alex, who if listening, was doing so only out of the corner of his ear.

"How'd you end up in Corning?"

"I'm still not sure about that and never happy to be there. George landed a contract to work with them on silicon wafers and fiber optics. It kind of became a base."

It seemed more of a deposition, than conversation, but I continued: "So how did you get to Cat?"

"Oh, that was through British Airways. One of our attendants had been there before, so I needed a few days away, heard it was a good place to relax. Alex invited me to go fishing with him one day. The rest, as they say, is history."

"How did your husband end up in Cat?"

"He should have been named "Curious George." I told him about Cat, which he looked up, and he became interested in Sandy Cay where they mine sand. We had divergent views on the use of sand."

She made sure her eyes caught mine and said: "He wanted it in a microscope. I wanted it under my ass."

I ignored the intentional innuendo and said: "Could he swim?"

"Never asked him?'

I turned to Alex who was off the phone and said: "What about you Alex, can you tell me anything more about him that you think might be helpful?"

He looked at his watch and said: "I better get you to the airport if you're going to catch your flight. It's Florida, you know, the roads around the airport are always under construction."

He got up, meaning the conversation was over. I said good bye to Mrs. Frampton, and then Dami on the way out. We got in Alex's Mercedes and made our way through the neighborhoods onto the Interstate to West Palm Airport. On the way we mainly talked about the weather, golf and fishing. I was hesitant to probe Alex's relationship with Mrs. Frampton, though I knew now I was not dealing with a grieving widow. I wasn't thrown off or even judgmental, I had plenty of evidence in my practice that widow's, more often than not, had sufficient reasons not to grieve. I said:

"Can you tell me anything else about George Frampton you might think is helpful?"

"Actually I didn't have much direct contact with him. I got wind somewhere that this guy was a whiz on silicon and I knew exactly where the best silicon in the world was being mined.

Near Cat at Sandy Cay. Mining and minerals I know something about. Computers, fiber optics and chips, I know nothing. He seemed like someone worth getting to know."

We were at the drop for my flight. Helping me get my bag from the trunk, he said: "Jake, don't read too much into Mrs. Frampton and me. Guys can get lonely. She and George were on the outs when I met her. Keep your eye on the prize here. The insurance company is stonewalling for some reason and the answer's not in Frampton's past."

"OK." Putting my bag down, saying to Alex: "Trina said she didn't know whose name the boat was titled in when it sank. You or the company."

He said: "It doesn't matter, does it? I am the company Jake. Let me know how you make out. I'd like to see this wrapped up soon."

He shook my hand, got in the Benz and drove off. I picked up my bag and walked into the airport thinking that it was hard to not let the smooth talk fool you.

Chapter Eleven

—

The flight from West Palm to Greater Pitt was uneventful with only a few minutes for the airport pastime of people watching: the small time business man validating himself by cell phone, overweight midriff exposed Harley moms, and the young Caribbean vacationers travel agencies hire to strut around. Bryan had called saying to stop on the way through Pittsburgh as he had more information. We arranged to meet at Permanti Brothers on the Strip. I asked Bryan to get him to get some background on Frampton and Tad Industries, as I needed information. Eva had set up a meeting later in the day with Bert Tad of Tad Industries located near Ligonier.

Walking into Permanti's, Bryan was elbows on the bar, pressing forward, locked in conversation with the waitress, hovering over his mussed fries and slab of beef, flattened in a dripping cole slaw sandwich. I moved his bush jacket from the stool beside him to the rack and sat down. I caught the waitress saying to Bryan: "Sure, but it will take me a minute." She walked away.

"What's that all about?" I said.

"I'm researching tattoos. She said it's a personality litmus test. It's not if you have one, but whether you want one. If you do, she thinks it means at some level you live life, not simply endure it. People who don't want one are usually more worried about their looks than those who do. Kind of the like the Harley motto: if you have to ask, you wouldn't understand. It comes out when they say: 'What would it look like when I get old. What will my grandma think.' Hell, grandma probably has one!"

"Are you getting one?"

"I don't know. I just started the research."

"Does she?"

"Yeah. On the base of her back. I'm thinking L-4, L-5. It's a little angel. Says it looks out for her. She hasn't let anyone see it yet. Makes it kind of special, wouldn't you say?"

What I didn't say, but thought was: How does this little nerd get people to confide in him all the time?

The waitress came back bringing me an Iron and handing Bryan a note. He put it in his pocket without comment.

"What do you have for me?" I said.

He reached down to his satchel and pulled out a stack of papers, handing them to me. I looked at the top page which was a web page and shifted through others which included print outs of newspaper articles, web articles and magazine pieces. "How about a summary?"

"Sure." He proceeded, between the falling fries and slaw: "Most of what I have is from the webpage for Frampton's consulting company. The site has attached a number of articles he's authored. Some pretty neat stuff. The focus is on the medium to put the chip in, mainly silicon."

I interjected: "Thus the title: "Silicon Medium Consultant.""

"Exactly. You can read through, but if you like I can tell you about the two lead articles."

"That would be good." I took a sip of beer thinking one thing Permanti Brothers did well was serve ice cold bottled beer.

Bryan continued: "The one article was on artificial intelligence, AI. The stuff of science fiction, the computer that thinks for itself, Big Blue with a personality, HAL from 2001, A Space Odyssey. Frampton's theory is that AI is going nowhere until the silicon base is more developed, a platform or superstructure, that would allow the circuits, the chip, to develop on its own. To not only rewire itself, but to make itself grow, to expand within the structure, to grow intellectually, at literally a sub-atomic level."

Bryan took two swigs as if getting ready for something big: "I'll tell you Jake, it does seem weird. It's not that the guy is off track. What he's writing is not new, it's more repackaged. But he gets a lot of mainstream press coverage without a lot of qualifications. I put in two Wall Street Journal articles, one by a brokerage firm, mentioning Frampton by name. You know what silicon chips are made from?"

"Not really."

"Actually it's silicon dioxide, the second most common element. But, no matter. Sand my good friend. Sand. Same stuff glass is made of. That's what probably led him to Corning. The rumors are Frampton had quite a few contracts with Corning and they have some unresolved issues."

I looked at the clock on the wall, neon green Rolling Rock, and said: "I have a meeting with Tad Industries in about an hour and half. I need to get going. Anything you can tell me about Tad?"

He ordered another Iron City, quite unusual for Bryan, and proceeded to tell me what he had about Tad. Tad Industries was owned by the Tad family, principally Burt Tad. Burt, in his eighties now, started the business when he graduated from Oxford, after six good years at Yale, followed by another six traveling the world. Those travels, to often uncommon places, he parleyed into exclusive franchises with foreign governments, supplying whatever was needed, from stamps to cars. His emphasis was "branded" products and the right to sell the product in that country. Coke and Pepsi toothpick holders were big. Bryan added that it was difficult to get any public information about Tad Industries. I asked if there was any Bahaman connection and he wasn't sure, but figured there was one. He reached into his pocket and handed me a raised plastic stamp with the face of the King Edward, Duke of Windsor, with the seal of the Bahamian government under it, and thirty cents in the right corner. He picked it up on the internet at a web site connected to Tad Industries. One of many little side lines Tad had still producing income.

I told Bryan I had to get going, and so did he. On the way out I asked him what the note from the waitress was about. He said: "I asked her to write down the name of the tattoo parlor."

He handed me the note which read: *Mary Ann's Tattoos, Oakland.* Then under that she wrote: *If you want to be the first to see my angel fly, call me.*

"You getting a tattoo?"

"Don't know.   I have to do some more research.   I don't think I'll show Nicole the note though."

I said: "Good idea."

Chapter Twelve

J ust out of Pittsburgh, I accessed America's first "super-highway", Pennsylvania's most dangerous byway, "The Turnpike", toward Route 30 East to Ligonier. Ligonier, once Lt. George Washington's army proving ground, is now best known for Arnie's Army and his Laurel Valley "Pink Jacket" Golf Course. Bert Tad's estate and offices were nestled in the Rolling Rock countryside up a slightly hidden driveway leading to a red brick pillared country estate house. The driveway meandered past a white and red vintage British fighter jet parked in the yard, which I would be told later was a gift from the British Secretary. I parked in front of the open doors of the attached four bay garage, housing three Rolls Royce's and a 1980's Lincoln Town Car with a silver dog ornament on the front of the hood, the latter being Bert Tad's favorite means of inconspicuous, by his standards, mode of transport. As I got out a small elderly man, slightly hunched over, was coming from the side of the house. Greeted with a smile Bert Tad welcomed me to Tad Estates. We walked inside, through the kitchen and past the black maid who was reading Star magazine while watching the compact TV on the counter. Passing through hallways, dodging artifacts, sculptures and antiques, we entered a spacious two story three fire-placed living room.

"Can I get you a drink, Mr. Quinn? I'm having a whiskey, myself. Takes the edge off."

Marveling at the balcony that ran the entire length of the gymnasium size room, I said: "That would be fine."

"Good Irish man. Can't deny your heritage, Mr. Quinn." He said seemingly pleased he had a drinking partner for afternoon. He brought us the drinks, not the least bit small, from the wet bar in the corner. He sat down on the couch across from me, saying:

"So what do I owe the honor of meeting with Alex Beck's attorney?"

"Alex asked me to help an acquaintance of his look into some problems with an insurance policy involving a boating accident. I really don't know if you can help or not."

"I've known Alex a long time. We've traded enough favors that I've lost count who is ahead or behind. I don't have many years left, I sure would like to be on the plus side. What do you need? Can I get you another drink first?"

Turning my glass to the light from the far window, I said: "Not yet. But if you don't mind me asking what's the brand?"

"Tullamore Dew, Irish Whiskey." Said as if telling me a secret, showing me the bottle. "Don't go Irish and get the cheap stuff though. Get the Twelve Year stock."

He came back to the couch waiting for me to speak. I said: "You know Alex has a place in the Bahamas?"

"Been there many times. Seems like another life, yet yesterday. Heady days. Bebe Rabozo, Nixon, Lyndon Johnson. They all came to Cat." He paused, reflecting, taking a measure of his former self maybe. "Johnson. Son of a bitch, bigger than life. Great man. Great drinker. Tormented. Fate. Karma. Destiny. They're all the same." He looked more directly at me. "Do you think you control your fate, Mr. Quinn?."

"I suppose not."

No response to my answer. He caught me giving him that look you give the elderly when you're not sure if they're really talking to you or themselves.

"Where were we?" He said.

I tried to cover the gap quickly. "The boat that sank was Alex's new Merritt. I'm just following up on some information about a dive boat that's been off Alex's side of Cat for quite some time now. Probably nothing, but the crew and boat are being rented out of Bimini and paid for by Tad Industries. I thought maybe you or someone in your company might have gotten some feed back on the accident."

He put his drink down, a narrowing of the eyes, a slight frown and a nodding of the head. He got up and walked to the corner of the room that led to a long hallway and yelled:

"Diane. Can you come here please?"

He said to me: "Diane will be here and we'll see if there's something a foot I'm not aware."

From the hallway came a forties attractive slightly heavy woman, dressed pleasantly, with page boy styled blonde hair. Walking across the living room, steno pad in hand, she said, not formally, but politely: "Yes, Mr. Tad."

"Diane, this is Jake Quinn, who works with our good friend Alex Beck. He drinks Tullamore Dew also."

She stepped toward me, with hand out: "With that I'm sure you're now a friend of Mr. Tad. How do you do Mr. Quinn?"

I said, getting up, trying to wipe the moisture from my hand holding the drink to greet hers: "Fine. Please call me Jake."

I sat back down with Diane remaining standing. Burt Tad said: "Do we have business activities right now in the Bahamas involving a dive boat from Bimini?"

She said firmly, no hesitation: "Not that I'm aware of."

"When was the last time we had anything going on there?"

"I can check the exact date, but the only contract we have is to supply stamp machines to their postal system in Nassau. Do you need to see the contract?"

"No. No. Thanks, Diane."

She nodded a good bye to me and Tad and went back the hallway which I assumed led to the offices of Tad Industries. Tad said to me, waiving his drink: "Let me know when you need another. So where did you get this information about my company being on Bimini?"

I saw no reason not tell him what I knew: "The invoices from the dive company referenced Tad Industries. I guess I'll check it out further. Maybe they were mistakes."

"Do that, will you? But keep me informed, because if my name is being used then I'll need to make some phone calls to certain people who should know better."

Tad stood up, walked over to the wet bar and made himself another Dew, and then ambled over to a large photo on the wall, staring at it. The photo was of a handsome young man and pretty woman dressed in Safari fashion, sitting cross legged, taking part in what seemed to be a royal Asian ceremony.

58

Taking a sip, he said:

"Mr. Quinn. This photo is of my wife Susie and me taken many years ago in Siam. Thailand now."

He walked away from it, and I expected a story, in fact, wanted to hear it, curious to know what the world was like before the globe got smaller. But he didn't continue. "Let's take a walk."

I said, holding my glass up, "Refill?"

He nodded and smiled. Getting me another drink, throwing an extra splash in his, he took me on a tour of his estate and offices. Diane and another secretary had offices down the hallway into a basement area. Outside we walked through the old horse barns, now empty stalls, then up an old horse trail to the top of a hill overlooking the Rolling Rock valley to the west. He stood looking out. He said:

"Mr. Quinn, if you don't mind, I'm going to let you walk yourself back. I think I'll stay up here awhile. Susie and I came here and picnicked when we came back from Siam. A prince with his princess."

I simply nodded an affirmation of my leaving and turned to walk back. A few steps down the path, he said: "Alex Beck is no saint. Nor is he even loyal to a fault. Neither am I for that matter. I'm getting too old for any more intrigue, but I still have some fight left in me. I don't like people using my name. I'll let you know if there's something you need to know."

I said: "Thanks for your time. And the drink."

I was turning away again and he said: "I like you Quinn. Have you ever been fox hunting?"

"Can't say I have."

"I've learned that if someone makes a monkey out of you, they expect you to act like a monkey. They're not prepared when you turn out to be a fox."

I said: "I'll keep that in mind."

He turned back to his view. I walked down the hill, past the silent Rolls Royce's and once thundering jet, now still.

Chapter Thirteen

———

Abraham Lincoln said a lawyer's stock and trade is his time and advice. That and a pair of testicles. I didn't give much advice the next week, mainly cleaning up files and preparing an argument before a judge who had never tried a case while in practice, but was fully prepared to enlighten me on how to try mine. A fairly common occurrence. I reviewed emails from Trina's staff about a series of mine inspections at company sites that had her concerned. In the evenings I read the articles Bryan provided on Frampton and did some internet searching myself. After understanding the corporate maze and divisions at Corning, I had Eva set up a meeting with William Langewestle for later in the week. According to a note Bryan had written on the side of an article, Langewestle was most likely Frampton's contact at Corning.

The night before leaving for Corning I had a few Yuenglings at the local watering hole, Murdock's. Staring at the Speed channel on the corner screen I mulled over whether Bert Tad was being up front with me about the Bahamas. His secretary Diane's seemingly unrehearsed answers appeared genuine. I got a six pack of Rolling Rock to go. When I got back to the office a red scarf was hanging over the door knob and a Lexus was parked in the driveway. I picked up the scarf as I opened the door, which I thought I had locked, walked through the office and up the old servant steps to my apartment. Candles were lit in the foyer and living room, with Candie Daffler's saxophone playing softly in the background. The foyer was also the entrance to the kitchen on my right where my feminine intruder was washing dishes. It was Trina. She turned to me: "Have you ever thought of a maid?"

"Don't you knock?"

"Not when I have a key."

She came over and gave me a hug and a kiss, which I accepted and returned, wondering what she was doing here, but had no reason to ask because I knew she would tell me soon enough. I said: "How's OB?"

"So-so. They transferred him to rehab. The doctor said he'll be ok, but it's going to take awhile."

"Did you hear anymore about who was chasing us?"

"No."

She put her dish towel down: "Can we talk business?"

"Sure, I can't pay you more than a five an hour for the dishes but if you have something else in mind, let me know the price?"

"Funny. Did you read the email we sent you?"

"Yes."

"Well. What's your reaction?"

The subjects were issues with the Pennsylvania Department of Environmental Protection, known simply as DEP, on natural gas wells the company had dotted throughout the area and on some coal stripping operations. Three inspections on different gas well locations and two coal inspections in one week. Each time the inspector had pulled the permit, survey maps, production records and, most unusually, interviewed the land owners asking whether there were any "problems" to report. No citations were given out, but the inspector told the well tenders that he would be back, and everything better be in order.

I said: "Who was the inspector? Decker?"

"Yeah, he was one of them. But Fantera was the other."

Thomas Decker was a former surface mining inspector who had harassed a fair number of operators out of business and since there were now more coal inspectors than miners, they moved him over to more fertile ground, gas well sites. Decker was notorious for nit picking, and in his spare time attending Sierra Club meetings. Decker lacked credibility in court, but that was not the case with Fantera.

Joe Fantera was an old high school friend who operated a D-9 dozer before going to college and, unable to get employment back in the coal industry, was "forced" to work for DEP. He worked with companies, knew the good from the bad and was reliable, and didn't view owners as having targets on their backs. If he cited, someone had screwed up and in the long run it prevented a potential impending disaster or uncontainable fine. He was not liked inside DEP at the state level, but much appreciated at the district and local level, as they had a better understanding of the need to regulate, but not destroy viable companies. Eight more insufferable years and he would have his retirement and health benefits, if he didn't implode from boredom before that.

I said: "Did you talk to Joe."

"Sort of. He was very uncomfortable. Very sheepish. Almost embarrassed that he couldn't talk much about it, just that everything better be in order. All business. He had federal inspectors with him."

We both knew that on-site federal inspections were almost unheard of. Although many of the environmental mandates were federal, the feds had turned over enforcement to the states twenty years ago. The feds role was now more inspecting the state inspectors, in between attending "important" seminars in western resorts and spas and returning to the mother ship in Washington, D.C. on occasion.

I said: "They haven't cited you yet."

Her face had an incredulous look. She said: "Come on Jake. It's just a matter of time. They've got jobs to justify. If they want to shut us down it's a given. The profit margins on coal are razor thin, and a two or three week shut down fighting DEP bullshit kills us for the year."

"What did Kim have to say about it?"

"I didn't call her yet."

Kim was Kimberly Hallston, state representative in Harrisburg. Kim had been a fairly low key county commissioner then ten years ago the former representative stumbled and his party, of course, disavowed any knowledge of his existence. She ran as an independent and slipped in. She was Chair of the Environmental end of the DEP Subcommittee. She couldn't tell DEP what to do, but she could get information, and fast. I would have thought Trina had already called her, particularly with the amount of money Trina had invested in her.

She continued: "I don't need to call in a favor yet, particularly if this goes nowhere. Besides I'm not even sure this is a state issue. We've got problems at sites in New York as well."

She paused, coming up beside me, moving her hips against my leg, then saying with a smile: "In fact, that's the great thing about our relationship Jake. I don't need to call in favors with you. I can just hire you. Eva says you're on to Corning tomorrow or the next day. She wouldn't tell me what for, but my guess it's about Frampton. So it's the company's dime. On the way I've arranged for us to stop and talk to Joe Fantera and then we go on to Corning. You have business there, so do I."

"Just like that you're coming along?"

"Just like that." She said.

Then, with a flirting smile: "But, hey, I owe you for the night's lodging here. I'm sure we could work out some exchange."

I wanted to tell her to find some other lackey to order around, but didn't. A common denominator was waiting for us in the bedroom.

Chapter Fourteen

Trina, operating on her time line, no one else's, had a meeting already set up for eight-thirty the next morning with Joe Fantera at the Cochran coal site job. We always traveled well together, throwing our travel bags in her Lexus, while carrying accompanying mugs of tea. Our packing would have looked like an ad for the "Travel Smith".

The last time I had seen Joe Fantera was for a deposition three years ago defending Trina in a wrongful discharge lawsuit filed by a former geologist. People are drawn to the soft side of business men, and the tough side of business women. I learned then how tough Trina could be.

The case started when word got back to Trina that a company geologist, originally hired by Alex questioned her decision on water treatment procedures on a gas well site near state game lands. The geologist had concerns about the proximity of the well to a nearby swamp, referencing it as a wetland. Trina reviewed his report and concluded the area had not been declared wet lands and wanted the reference deleted. The geologist objected and implied in an in-house email that he felt an obligation to report the change to DEP if she did not at least make a statement that it was a "potential" wet land. When that email showed up on her screen, Trina marched down the hall to his desk and fired him on the spot. Several months later he filed a whistle blowing wrongful discharge lawsuit in federal court claiming environmental concerns should override the discharge an employee at will. The firing had surprised everyone in the company as he was the person most responsible for finding new gas fields, running from Williamsport to Corning, New York. The company commitment to the project was huge, with the potential return equally large. Everyone thought the geologist was critical to the project. Trina knew loyalty was more critical.

A jury never heard the case as it was dismissed after we produced several experts to confirm Trina's decision that it was not wet lands. In preparing the case, we discovered the employee had sent a blind copy of his objecting email to Alex. I suspected that was the real point for the firing. Trina's message was clear to the entire company: It was Trina's show. Disloyalty would not be tolerated.

On our trip out to the Cochran job we talked about Fantera. Fantera's dad and his uncle Nick had come to this country from Italy as boys, as my grandfather had from John Bull's Other Island. Mining coal and transporting by rail gave them their freedom. The media's negative spin on coal was not effective against Fantera's dad's generation, but I could see even Fantera was slipping into the environmental bureaucracy. Coal was no longer "black gold."

Fantera's off-white government issue Jeep Cherokee was just off a block of coal exposed in an ever moving pit, cutting across the Cochran farm. The sign next to the Jeep read: "Blast Area." Even with enough regulations in force to keep an army of technocrats in business to the next century, DEP still rarely shut a job down. The coal business had been reduced to such an extent that if they pushed, they would eliminate the industry in its entirety, and thus their jobs. Trina was right in wondering why the sudden interest in her job sites.

I pulled up behind the Jeep and Trina was out her door before we even stopped.

"Joseph." She said as she walked straight toward him and put out her hand. He grinned slightly and put his hand out, which she grasped and gave him a smile to die for. She said to him as I got out of the car:

"How's Jane?"

"She's good Trina." He said.

"Is the spa working out? I told Janie I would get up there last month but never made it. She was supposed to send me some cards. Make sure she does. How's Uncle Nick?"

"I'll tell Jane you asked about her and Uncle Nick's ok."

"Did he see that doctor at UPMC in Pittsburgh I talked

about?"

"Yeah, thanks." He turned to me. "Hey, Jake. Good to see you. Does Trina run your life as well or just us DEP lackeys?"

I shook his hand saying: "Oh, don't think you're special, Joe, she runs everyone's life. Males at least. Do you have any female inspectors, I would like to see how she does with them?"

I got a look from Trina on that one and she said, directed to Joe: "He's just the driver, ignore him. Let's take a walk, Joseph."

Trina led Joe away walking toward the edge of a highwall, with Trina's voice fading as they moved out of earshot. I went over to the side of the Lexus and stood there for about five minutes, watching D-9 bulldozers square up a block of coal, a highlift loading it out. My cell rang and I reached in picking it up from the seat, flipping it open:

"Attorney Quinn? Bert Tad here. Your secretary gave me your cell number, if that was alright?' "Sure. I told her to. What's up?" I said too casually for the respect I had for a man that much my senior.

"I would like to talk to you concerning the matters we discussed last week. I'm wondering if you could meet with me. Perhaps for your own good as soon as possible."

Not liking that last comment, without hesitation or maybe thought, I recited an old Firesign Theater line: "Don't worry, danger is my middle name."

He disregarded my comment and said: "Perhaps I'm overreacting but I want to talk to you about the Bahamas."

"I'm headed to New York later today and will be back I think tomorrow and probably could see you then."

"That's fine. I will be at your office two days from today at 9:00 am., if that's alright."

"See you then Mr. Tad."

I clicked off and a message flag came up. Bryon had called, saying to call him on his cell before I talked to anyone at Corning. I dialed Bryon and he answered, not with hello, but an enthusiastic: "Jake, found out some more about your missing Frampton. Did you read the articles I gave you?"

"Yeah."

"Good. It was a waste of time. Here's what I found out through the old grapevine as they say. It's true he wrote a bunch of stuff about artificial intelligence and silicon, but I don't think that's why they had him under contract at Corning. There's a legendary tech scientist named Stanford Ovonsky. Old Stan, close to 80 now, had the most creative concepts to come out of Silicon Valley, but never made any money because someone was always stealing his ideas. Stan's last big project was working on a chip called 'morph'. A code name the military attached to it. They're interested in anything that will make processors smaller. They're putting money into Corning's Research and Development. The techies now call the whole field: Ovonics. He's been working on this since the 60's. The material that changes from a disordered, amorphous, atomic state to a crystalline, from highly fluid to highly ordered structure."

"You're losing me Bryan."

"Really, you sound clear, is it your phone?"

"No, you idiot. I'm not following what you're telling me. What difference does it make to the chip?"

"Oh. Don't be silly, I don't even understand it. Maybe no one does, but Stan. The simple explanation is that when this morphing material changes back and forth, during the phases, it generates the ones and zeros for the digital products. And it doesn't need any power source."

"So?"

"Christ! It's a permanent rewritable chip that will last forever and you can put the files of the Pentagon on a chip the size of a postage stamp. Frampton's literature says he used to work with Stan in the 80's."

"So why do I need this information for my meeting with Corning?"

"Corning's got a team of investigators backtracking Frampton's actions over the last nine months. I'm guessing now, but I think they're wondering if Frampton wasn't using them and trying to get to some of Corning's proprietary information in fiber optics and silicon."

"So you're thinking Corning is meeting me to find out what I know, not the other way around."

"That's my guess."

I could see Trina heading to my car, with Joe already getting into his Jeep. I said: "Look, I got to go. Anything else real quick?"

"That's it in a nutshell."

"Ok, boss."

As I clicked off, Trina came around the car, with Joe pulling away. Trina said, curtly: "Let's go.'

"Sure, Miss Daisy."

We picked up Interstate 80 ten miles north and headed east then north to Corning. Thoughts were kept to ourselves the first hour or so. Trina finally said later: "So who were you talking to on your cell?"

I lied without hesitation. "Client. What'd you find out from Joe?"

"Not much."

"What's up with the enforcement?"

"He's not sure. But he's getting pressure from all levels. Says he has to play this very straight."

"Like he's ever played it any other way?"

Trina said with a raised tone: "Hey, Joseph only cites when he has no other choice. He's backed down my father many times, usually for his own good. Of course, my father had a hard time seeing it that way. He hasn't had non-paranoid thought in twenty years."

"So who's pushing it?"

"Like I said, he doesn't know and I'm not pressing him any further. I have other sources. I'll just keep climbing up the bureaucratic ladder until I find out. Then someone will pay."
All said with no smile, just a statement of future fact.

I lowered my imaginary chauffeur's cap. I drove the remainder of trip under a conversational yellow caution flag.

Chapter Fifteen

—

My meeting with William Langewestle from Corning's Photonic Technology Department was scheduled for four in the afternoon. We rolled into Corning at about three and checked into the local old time hotel that every town or city has, this one named The Stuben. Trina dropped me at Corning Headquarter just down the street and then she headed to meet with her landman, about a forty minute drive north. She said she would be back by dark. I did not know much about her New York gas operation, except they had been thumping the ground for about two years, finally drilled and hit some exceptional locations. The gas still had to be piped to market and within the last several weeks, at about the same time as her problems in Pennsylvania cropped up, a major snafu developed with a right of way. Trina's landman was going to bring her up to date and they had a meeting scheduled with one of the now disgruntled owners.

I walked into the lobby of Corning headquarters, a blend of old and new buildings, with, hard to guess, a lot of glass. Bryan told me that Corning was truly on the "cutting edge", as much as he hated that term, of fiber optic and anything that moved data quicker, inside or outside the internet. But they were being bypassed by the wireless movement, just like their northern brethren at Kodak by digital. Photonics, which Langewestle headed, was under pressure to find a new market, or create one.

With directions from the receptionist, I made my way toward the Photonic Technology Department and to Langewestle's office, a throw back to the 1970's. Langewestle was about forty-five, tall, thin, dressed in a business suit, looking like he played some tennis in his time, probably a serve and volley man. As I walked in Langewestle got up from his chair where he was conferring with another gentlemen at a table. Their conference table was near the inside windows that overlooked an expansive floor of cubicles and research cubby holes.

"Mr. Quinn," Langewestle said. "Thanks for taking the time to meet with me. This is a colleague of mine, Dr. Gerald Stine. He worked with Mr. Frampton. I hope you don't mind if he sits in?"

Stine got up to shake my hand. Stine was mid-sixties, short, portly, curly grey black shoulder length thinning hair, half mustache, dressed in blue jeans and a khaki jacket. There was a pipe peeking out of his coat pocket.

Doctor of whatever Stine said sharply, looking Langewestle's way: "I wouldn't say "worked with Frampton.""

Not ignoring the quote or acknowledging it, Langewestle said: "Mr. Quinn, have a seat."

After some pleasantries about the trip and offer of beverage, Langewestle continued: "Gerry here was not in favor of the contract we had with Frampton and often we ask managers to oversee a project they might not approve. Adds a layer of objectivity to its oversight. Did you know Frampton, Mr. Quinn?"

I avoided a direct answer until I could see how forthcoming they were going to be on our first date, so to speak. I said: "In the last month I've been working with his wife on their insurance policy."

With that I caught Stine give Langewestle a glance, with Langewestle providing no conspiratorial nod or response, the understood lack of expression that comes so natural to engineers. It's not that engineers aren't people persons, they just like thinking about things and ideas more than people. They'll think about people if they interfere with a problem to solve and apparently Frampton was a problem worth thinking about.

"Actually I met Mrs. Frampton several times myself, but mostly after her husband disappeared." Stine added.

"Missing or dead?" I said.

"I guess we have the same question, Mr. Quinn. We were hoping you could tell us a little more about what happened to him."

70

I said: "I'll tell you what I can, but you may know more than I do. Can I ask first what his relationship with Corning was?"

"Gerry." Langewestle said looking over to his colleague.

Stine said: "We saw Frampton's articles show up in some tech journals, nothing spectacular, but it looked like he was bumping into some ideas we were working on. As you can guess Mr. Quinn, we can't relate all the details we were working on, but our Research and Development people started to get interested in his work on ovonics some time last year. We read he worked with Ovonsky which we took as some level of credibility. After a bunch of email exchanges the geniuses at R&D hastily, in my opinion, contracted with him as an independent."

"What was he like in person? Your gut reaction." I said.

Stine said, with a hint of delight: "Never met him. Never met anyone in this building who did."

Langewestle interceded: "Don't get the wrong impression Mr. Quinn. It is not unusual to not have a face to face with our contractors. How many times have you dealt in legal matters, over maybe months, and never meet the other lawyer?"

Langewestle defense for not meeting Frampton rang true, but the tone was rehearsed, probably the same argument he might have had to make to the CEO. I nodded an agreement and he said: "Sometimes our R&D can get stuck in their box. We look for creative minds inside and outside Corning."

I said: "So exactly what did he have a contract for?"

Stine said: "Mr. Frampton had some powerful friends in Washington. He came to us with government clearances that frankly no more than a handful of our people have. We supplied him with some very sensitive Corning data and access to our research. He had this access through an encrypted Palm Pilot. The hope was that with whatever access he had to government information, along with his knowledge and contacts, that he could help us solve the limitations on silicon and glass as a medium."

Langewestle said: "It was a crap shoot, but that's what R&D is sometimes. Viagra started out as heart medication."

I thought it a soft analogy, but hard to argue against. Stine, not liking the constant interruptions, and now seeming as agitated as an engineer could get, said: "Frampton in eight months produced nothing. We want the palm pilot back and whatever else he took."

The curly little troll obviously thought I had the palm pilot on me. Attorneys are used to the transposition: the lawyer's in on it. I smiled at Stine to rattle him, trying to make it into a smirk, suggesting I had his Maltese Falcon in the truck of my car.

I initially thought there was nothing I would reveal to Corning, but I sensed Stine was busting at the seams to dump on Frampton, just needing a nudge.

I said: "From talking to Mrs. Frampton I got the impression matters were not completely settled with her husband and Corning, I don't know, maybe some money due?"

Stine took the bait: "The nerve. Mrs. Frampton is sadly, sadly mistaken. The R&D allotment had a specific draw down, and out of the five hundred thousand allotted, one hundred and twenty-five thousand was drawn down before he came up missing. All invoices were paid to that date. Did she suggest to you we owed her more? How much?"

"Like I said, it was just an impression. I'll ask her."

Langewestle said: "When you do Mr. Quinn, you may want to ask whether she knows the whereabouts of the Corning Palm Pilot that her husband had in his possession at the time of his disappearance."

"I'll certainly will, but what makes you think she even knows anything about it? I didn't get the idea she knew a lot about what her husband did."

Stine opened one of the folders on the table, leafed through some papers and tossed several my way saying: "Here are copies from our accounting department's original draw down on the Corning/Frampton project account. You'll see that all these checks are written to Silicon Medium Consultants, all endorsed by Mrs. Frampton only. The second sets are direct electronic transfers into an account in Mrs. Frampton's name alone. Those draws and transfers are only possible using our Palm Pilot."

I moved the papers aside and said: "That doesn't mean she knew anything, just that she drew down."

Stine continued, even louder: "Come on, Quinn. You lawyers are all alike."

I said, staring at Stine: "An emotional engineer. There's an oddity."

Langewestle interceded again: "We never seemed to be able to get a hold of Frampton for a meeting. I met several times with Mrs. Frampton. When I had questions, I often talked or met with her, not Frampton. He always seemed out of town. Neither I, nor Dr. Stine, are suggesting she understood the research or the ideas, but I had the feeling she ran the show."

I said: "What do they say: dead men tell no tales."

Stine said: "If they're dead."

Langewestle cut him off saying: "Back to the Palm Pilot. We want it back. If we have to pay to get it back, well, that can be discussed."

Stine looked incredulous at that comment. He got out of his seat and walked to the end of the room.

Langewestle continued: "Frankly, Mr. Quinn, Washington has put us on notice that they are looking into it and that we are accountable under the Patriot's Act if there is any sensitive material unaccounted for. We would just as soon not go there."

"I'll ask her about the palm pilot, but my guess is that it is at the bottom of the ocean with Frampton."

Stine wanted back in the game, couldn't help himself, walked back and said: "That pilot and our codes are not at the bottom of the god damn ocean unless Neptune knows the access codes. Three days ago someone accessed the account and drew down the rest of the money and transferred it into an off shore account somewhere. Our investigators are working on that. Ask your client about that too Quinn."

Friends can call me by my last name. Often do. With acquaintances, I tolerate it. With strangers, it pisses me off. I gave the kind of stare that if at a bar you better be ready to kick ass or get your ass kicked. The old fart blinked first and started putting files back in his case. After that there was quite a bit of silence in the room. Seems that both parties had provided more information than they wanted but that usually is the case in personal meetings. We talked a while longer but it was clear that the substance was behind us. They agreed to let me know if they found out anything further and said I would convey any information about the palm pilot if I found anything. Business lies. There would be no further communication.

I walked back toward the hotel wondering if I had made a serious mistake in concocting that Mrs. Frampton was owed money. How the hell was I supposed to know about some off shore account or a missing three hundred and seventy-five thousand? I wanted a free ride for once on suspicions about my own client. Now I had legitimate reasons for reservations.

Before I made the hotel my cell phone rang.

"Mr. Quinn." It was a woman's voice.

"That's right, who is this?" Said with a puzzled tone as it was not a voice I was familiar with. I tended not to give my cell number out indiscriminately.

"This is Diane from Mr. Tad's office. Mr. Quinn, I see in Mr. Tad's appointment book that he was scheduled to meet with you the day after tomorrow."

"At my office, I think around 9 or 10."

"We have it at 9. But Mr. Quinn, he won't be making the appointment. Mr. Tad was killed this afternoon in an automobile accident."

I couldn't identify my emotions but it's confusing to have just met someone and they die. As if I had something to do with it, but couldn't see how. I pictured Mr. Tad in his car. All I could think of saying was: "What happened?"

"All we know is that he was coming home from Laurel Valley Golf Course and his car went off the road, down an embankment. The coroner and police are still looking into it."

"I'm sorry to hear that. Please express my sympathies to the family."

"I will do that. Mr. Quinn, I need to tell you that Mr. Tad called the office, apparently after he wrecked. He sounded hurried but not hurt. He told me there was a dictation tape on his disk that I needed to type it and make sure you got it. And I was to tell no one about the call. He hung up before I could find out even where he was."

"Have you typed it yet?"

"I have the tape, but I have not yet had time to type it. There is too much going on here. In fact, I have to go right now."

"Thanks." And I added: "I'd be careful who you tell about that tape."

"I'll do that Mr. Quinn. There's much you don't know about Tad Industries. Be careful yourself."

Chapter Sixteen

My first thought after absorbing Tad's death was that I needed a drink. That reasonable controlling good society man loitering within fueled by all the boring non-drinkers sometimes talks you out of a cold one. Shouldn't need a drink. Might have a problem. I was thinking about that as I ordered my second Captain Morgan's, straight. I was sitting at the bar of The Jungle Room, down a side street from the Bistro where I had met Mrs. Frampton. The Jungle Room was not a bistro, not really a gin mill, more a working man's tavern, owned by a "Stush" or "Vin" or "Johnny", probably titled in his wife's name and bought with his almost legit workers compensation settlement.

The décor suggested Corning had a sports identity problem. The wall displays ran the gambit from the Orange Men of Syracuse, to the Jets, to the Bills to NASCAR. Bob Seger's "Down on Mainstreet" played lonely on the jukebox to a poster of Dale, Jr. No Jeff Gordan on these walls. The clientele appeared to be shift workers, union retirees and a few boys not unhappy that they didn't attend college, but resigned to a seven to three at Lowes, listening to country tunes that underestimated redneck hopelessness. Be home for dinner soon hon, and we'll still have time to make Mikie's Little League Game. Your mom's coming along too, great. Oh no, only had a couple. No shots, being a game day and all.

Could have been the second drink, or maybe I would have made the call later anyway, but I picked up my cell, stopped at MootCell, pressed, waited and in a few seconds heard:

"Quinnie, Moot."

I said, in two drink fashion: "What's happening? Where ya at?"

"Just sitting around here at Wally's, laying out some walleye."

"How they hitt'n?"

There was a pause, then his loud voice heard directed away from his cell: "Wallie, it's Quinn. Wants to know how they're hitting?"

I could just make out in the background: "Tell that lame fuck to get his ass up here and find out for himself."

Moot said: "Did you hear that?"

"Yeah, well, tell Wally that if he kept better company I'd be up more often."

"Wally's" was the only bait and fishing shop just off the harbor at Conneaut on the Ohio side of Lake Erie. Frank Mootaski, known as Moot, had found a summer hang out there about five years ago, living on his twenty-five footer, pursuing walleye and perch, while his wife remained happily at home running the dog kennel and grooming business. Moot's state police pension wasn't near enough to pay for all the boat fuel, dock fees, fishing gear and Old Milwaukee, consumed in one season. That spawned "Moot's Investigative Services", his private investigator business. I called on Moot every so often to run a plate, serve a paper, or investigate an accident. That and keep me in a supply of walleye.

I said: "Moot, you got time to look into an accident for me?"

"Well, how soon do you need it? The fishin's starting to heat up here. Hit every down rigger and plainer board today. The ten mile mark is red hot."

"ASAP would be good. It's down in the Ligonier area. If I remember right the DA there was a former trooper. I thought maybe you would know him."

"Otis Nageli. I was in the academy with him. What's going on in Ligonier?"

"I am not sure really if it is anything at all. Get a pencil and I'll give you some details."

Moot asked Wallie for a pencil and I gave him enough information on Tad to start snooping around. I told him to keep it simple, not to contact the family or business but ask around the courthouse and police. Maybe see the DA. Get the coroner's report if there was one, which I doubted being an auto accident. Moot said he would get back to me in couple days.

I was considering one more drink when my cell rang. Viewing the caller I.D., I said: "Trina. Where are you at?"

"About 50 miles from Corning. Where are you?"

"The Jungle Room."

She laughed: "Is that a chain?"

"Juke joint heaven, honey, wall to wall."

"Well, pace yourself so you don't go blind."

"Ok. Call me when get near town, I'm heading back shortly to the room. How did your meeting go?"

"Don't ask. I'll tell you later. See you in a little bit, you're breaking up."

I put the cell in my pocket and asked the bartender where "Garden Circle" apartments were. He said: "Garden Circle. About three blocks from here. Go out the front, make a right, can't miss'm."

"My niece is thinking of renting there, what do you think of the place?"

"How old is she?"

"Oh, Linne's about thirty."

"Well, Mac" he said "Corning built them in the 60's and they were for their upper management guys. Then very exclusive and pricey. Pensioners and widows now. Can't afford to move. The neighborhood's not bad. It'd be safe, but not much action for a young lady."

I thanked him, left a tip and followed the path he had laid out until I saw the small sign for "Garden Circle Apartments", a vacancy sign hung underneath. It was an old red brick, five stories, old windows, few air conditioners sticking out, and no landscaping. A set of glass doors led into the lobby. I walked in to an area originally designed as a hotel lobby and scanned the list of apartments. Some with names, some not. "218" still had "Frampton" on it.

An abandoned reception desk had a sign that read: "For information go to Office at end of hall." Seeking information, I obeyed and found at a desk an elderly lady with washed out white blond hair speared and in a bun. Her lip stick so badly missed the mark, she could have put it on with her feet. She smiled up at me and said: "Can I help you young man?"

"Yes. I wanted to see Elizabeth Frampton."

"Elizabeth Frampton, the British woman." She said, not so much with a frown but an acknowledgement that she knew an Elizabeth Frampton. Before I said anything further, she said: "And what is your name?"

"Rodger Conrad. I'm a friend of hers. She had a package for me and said to go to the desk to get it if she wasn't in."

"There's no package here."

"Oh. Could you tell me where she works or might be at this time so I could find her?"

"Mr. Conrad, she left here last week and turned her key in. I cleaned the apartment out myself. It was mess if you ask me. I don't know how one woman can't keep an apartment clean. As fussy as the British are."

"Her husband George has kind of a slob."

"Well, I never met him." Saying that with a tone I couldn't catch.

"Sorry to bother you." I said.

As I turned to leave, she said: "She said Goodwill was going to come and get her stuff, but I had to haul it to the shed out back. You're welcome to look out there for it. And when you're done how about doing an old lady a favor and take it over to Goodwill on South Tenth Street?"

"Sure. Where's the shed?"

"It's around back. Not locked."

Her facial expression made me think she wanted to tell me something more, so I said: "Isn't that just like Elizabeth to tell you one thing and do another?"

She smiled at that, pulling the pencil from her hair, and pointing it at me: "Mister, I can't say she'll be missed here at Garden Circle. I don't know much about her, but she sure was unfriendly, except maybe to some of her male suitors." She said that with just the right amount of small town distain Aunt Bea from Mayberry would have.

I thought of asking her some more questions, but her phone rang. From what I could tell, it was Mr. Patterson calling from

Apartment 50 to complain. Apparently, he didn't land at Normandy to put up with a leaking facet. Ike would hear about this. I nodded a good-bye, motioning with my hands that I would stop back and get the stuff. She nodded, ok.

Elizabeth, it'll slow you down having too much stuff.

Chapter Seventeen

—

I was standing on a corner leaning against a post in front of the Garden Apartments having conflicting thoughts on my client Frampton. Alex helped strays often, usually out of sentimentality, but never stray women. At least once a year, I prepared a guarantee for a bank loan for a old friend. The friend signed a note to Alex but it was superfluous, allowing the signer to keep his dignity. Default was a forgone conclusion, as was Alex paying the bank and not trying to collect. A small fee for Alex to pay to remind himself where he came from. But I never saw him mix business and pleasure when it came to women. I understood the sexual attraction and companionship, certainly from his angle, but hers? Was she a stray? Whose dog and pony show was this? Alex *and* Mrs. Frampton?

Eventually I made my way to the Stuben, changed into some ugly running attire and ventured down a few Corning side streets for a run. Back in thirty minutes, I opened the door and found lady's evening attire was spread out on the bed, the shower running. Not jumping immediately into the shower with her, and her not asking, said something about our current relationship. What, I didn't know. Although I was good at recognizing the symbolism of such events, I had little clue on how to interpret them. I did yell in though: "What's new?"

To which she said: "I'll tell you at dinner after a few drinks."

"OK." I waited for Trina to come out of the shower to towel off, watching the show and her letting me. Finally she pushed me aside: "Get cleaned up Rover. Dinner's in a half hour."

Showering as ordered, I got dressed, not saying much, as we both heard CNN's Lou Dobbs informing the masses how much longer it would take them to retire. Dinner reservations were across town at Kolos, a martini bar/restaurant. I was only slightly underdressed and Trina may or may not have been. She was a woman that set the tone walking into a room. Long glances from women, short stares from their husband. Somewhere into our second bottle of wine I asked her about her excursion.

"Let's say" she said "it was not mission accomplished."

I said cutely: "Your Boca Raton Versace style didn't wow'm over here in backwoods New York?"

"Save the sarcasm little man. Quite the contrary. McAlister, the landowner, was quite glad to see me. We talked about his right of way and he showed me the area that has been declared a wetland by the feds that is blocking us getting the pipeline out that will connect the well. Said the EPA has been there almost everyday. Taking tests, setting up posts, air samples, soil samples. You name it."

"I thought you were a wetlands expert. Is it a wetland or not."

"Not a chance. A highway was up graded five hundred feet from his line, was not culverted properly, has backed up with some water that crosses near where we need the line. That was about four years ago and now there are some tadpoles fornicating there, and a duck pees on occasion on his way to Florida. It's an enviro-nazis' dream."

"So bring in your Rainbow Warrior lawyers from New York and straighten'm out." I said showing once again my sense of inferiority to urban counsel.

Trina, shaking her head, said: "Jakie, Jakie, Jakie. The Environmental Hearing Board's a court in name only. You know that. It's a rubber stamp. If the feds have orders from DC, sure I could win, but not in my lifetime or probably my children's."

"So what's your plan?"

"I do not know right now. What do you think?"

That was hard to swallow. Trina was not one to take a defensive position and wait for the enemy. My guess: she was headed straight for Washington. So I said what she wanted to hear: "I'd get your engineering in line then call one of your insider friends and set up a meeting at the site."

82

"I already have the engineering done." She said. "I'm heading back to Florida to make sure dad's not somehow already involved."

"What's Alex had to do with it?"

"Come on. You should know your favorite client by now. If he thinks I have to make a real decision, he shows up somewhere. Usually with some prompting by Dean." She paused, tipping her wine glass to me for a refill. I sensed she was ready to move on and was right as she said: "What happened with you today on the Frampton mystery tour?"

"An enigma wrapped in a mystery? I don't know what I learned today. With your help, maybe we'll learn more tonight."

"Pray tell?" She said with a Raymond Chandler tone and big-eyed Betty Davis look. Or maybe it was Joan Crawford. I had seen an old Clark Gable/Joan Crawford movie and Joan seemed more devious than Betty. Maybe calculating is a better word.

I said: "I spoke to her landlady and fished around at her apartment complex. She pretty much kept to herself, with not much on the husband either."

"That's not odd behavior for a lady, using that term lousily, in a city. They keep to themselves, avoid eye contact. Like walking down the street, especially when their husbands aren't around and double that when dealing with, I assume, a nosey landlady."

"You're probably right. Anyway, she left a bunch of junk behind that I told the landlady we would take to Goodwill."

"We pay you legal fees for stuff like this? And I assume you expect me to go through another woman's personal belongings? Someone who you know I am not personally fond of, a gold digger at best."

"Yes."

"Drink up and let's get going." She said with a smile.

Rushing our eating, leaving the restaurant, driving to the back of the Garden Circle apartments making as little noise as possible as we pulled out a couple of plastic bags of loose clothes, and three or four cardboard boxes marked with a tag: Frampton/Goodwill. We left all the Ikea furniture pieces and two cheap rugs, the quality of which Trina took some pleasure in pointing out.

We headed back to the Stuben with our treasure and dumped the bags and boxes on the floor in the room. Trina said she would take the bags and I could open the boxes. Kids at Christmas we sat on the floor, her with the bags and me opening the boxes. Lady Sherlock held pieces up, checked tags, felt the material, and made facial expressions uninterruptible to men. I took out various books and knick-knacks and laid them out. Trina got up, went into the bathroom, washed her hands and said:

"I'll go first." Starting as if giving a corporate presentation, she said: "It's as if there are two women here." Pointing to her left. "This first stack came from the first bag. From the wrinkles, these clothes have been in that bag for awhile. All the tags are from England, none of them very expensive, department store, not designer. Stylish, conservative, wool, and drab. One curious item, stuck in a sweater, was a bra. Label, 35, b cup." Dangling it for my view.

I thought I got the drift of that remark, but didn't say anything. She continued: "Now, on our right," pointing dramatically, "we have some things more current. All these are equally conservative, all clothes you could pick up at Sears, Target, even Wal-Mart. In fact, a couple still had tags on them Marshals. Most really day to day clothes you would see a clerk or secretary wear."

Picking up a possibly radioactive bra with a coat hanger, she said: "The curious item here is another bra, with a broken snap. Red no less and guess what size?"

I shrugged.

"Come on, your fantasy size. A d cup. Our little lady has had herself retrofitted sometime since coming to the States."

Trina seemed proud of her detective work. "And one more thing. In one of the pockets were some tags for some clothes not in her bags. All these tags were clearly designer, and damn expensive. In fact, I'm a bit jealous of our lass."

She seemed to be done, so I said: "So what do you make of the clothes then."

"Like I said, two women. If all this is hers, this girl was making some big transitions in her life. And in the process I think putting on a show up here in Corning a lot different than the one she's staging for dear old dad."

I said: "Ok. Here's what I found. Not much. A couple baskets. A few purses. A toaster. A small microwave. Some plates, knifes, forks, kitchen stuff. Work out videos. Romance novels. Several P.D. James Mysteries. One George Penecano's. And these."

I handed them to Trina. Her look was as curious as mine. The books were: "Initial Public Offerings: Secrets of an Insider.", "Greco's right: Greed is Good.", "Ovanics and Nanotech into the Twenty-first Century." and "Paper Tigers: The Fundamentals of Group Presentations."

"So what do you make of her reading habits?" Trina said.

"I'm not sure they're hers first. Probably her husbands. She obviously didn't think she had much use for them now. What's your take?"

Trina said: "She's no Jane Bond. Whatever she's up to either she's not bright enough to cover her tracks, or in the big scheme of things, she has nothing to hide so why bother. I think she's just…"

"A gold digger." I interrupted.

She nodded: "Right. Just Alex's type." This time she had showed a different type of smile, a bitter one.

After a water saving shower, we shuffled through Mrs. Frampton's books reading each other bits and pieces. I read her an incomprehensible description of ovanics and Trina read dramatically from a romance novel. We worked on adding our own endings: *"She lay in the arms of the only man who knew her, feeling a joy so powerful it had to be sinful, knowing it would all end tomorrow when….he had the scheduled sex change operation"*, or *"…his wife would be home from Sturgis."* or *"…the price of Imclone reached 60."*

Eventually, the light went out. We laid in bed in each other arms in awkward silence, but it was nice. Trina said: "Why don't we play like little girls and little boys tomorrow. Just for a day."

I said, protectively: "I forgot how. I don't think I'm allowed."

She said: "I could teach you."

Everything I knew about the blues, I learned from Trina. I got a first rate education but I have to give credit where credit is due. She was an experienced teacher. I wasn't sure I wanted her to teach me anything else. I simply kissed her good night.

Chapter Eighteen

In the morning I dropped the key card off at the Stuben Hotel desk while Trina grabbed a couple apples and two teas from the continental. Trina had an early flight out of State College, Pennsylvania on a commuter to Philadelphia, with a direct to West Palm. She apparently thought this through sometime prior to dinner the night before, had called her secretary to make all the arrangements and informed me that morning. Included in the itinerary was driving her car back to her Pennsylvania office. No need to discuss a hired hands duties. All of which did not put me in the playful mood hinted at the night before.

The conversation to Happy Valley came from *her* side of *her* car. Trina was pissed at the government for interfering with her companies and yakked about it most of the way. Neither she nor Alex was adverse to regulation, more often than not using it to their advantage as smaller competitors lacked the staying power to comply and survive. I nodded when appropriate as a good chauffeur should. Our departure at the airport was awkward as I remained confused over our relationship. Intimacy requires replacing self protection with trust and our past relationship was a hurdle. We hugged and then oddly shook hands before she got on the plane. Business lovers? The only way to describe it. My caution was disproportionately rewarded when I noticed walking out the terminal that the Flight Information Board screen had her commuter not headed to Philadelphia, as she told me, but to Washington, D.C... I guess I let Trina's smooth talk fool me.

Eva, the gatekeeper, had let no one slip past her, so all was well when I pulled into the office. One curiosity she noted was a walk-in, always viewed with caution anyway. Very buff, her exact words, a young man in a casual business suit, formal and polite, asking for me, not wanting an appointment. She had told him she did not know when I would be back and he left without a card or even leaving his name. Had law book salesman or advertiser modis operandi, but suspicious, she checked the car plates out the window when he drove off, noting a similar looking suited man in the passenger side. The plates were either municipal or federal and she handed me a note with the license number written down.

I spent the next day on more office work, dictating odds and ends, but quickly losing concentration, drifting intermittently back to the Frampton file trying to lay out a plan. Moot called and said he had some tid bits for me, and had arranged a meeting with the Westmoreland District Attorney, Otis Nageli, for eight thirty the next morning, asking if I wanted to go along. He would pick me up at seven sharp. I agreed.

On time the next morning for our Greensburg trip, Moot told me some background on the DA and his confrontation with the State Police:

"First, I drove to the State Police headquarters to look at the accident report and they said it wasn't available yet. So I asked to talk to the Trooper in charge, waited a few minutes and out comes the Captain, not the sergeant or even the lieutenant. Tells me the Trooper who made the report wasn't in. Wanted to know why I *needed* to see the report. He knows I don't need a reason, but I went along and told him I was doing a report for an attorney. Then he says 'Who wants to know?' treating me like a traffic stop."

I said: "Did you tell him?"

"I was going to, but with his fuck'n tone, like he was commanding me to tell him, fuck that. I said: 'Look Captain, I'd like to but can't, so why don't you just go get the report.' He said, smoldering: 'Well, we're at an impasse cause I don't think I can do that right now.' So that's when I said 'Impasse, my ass, now just go get the fucking report, like a good little trooper.' And with that I shoved my retired State Police I.D. and my $39.99 Detective Badge in his face."

"Did you get the report?" I injected.

"He gave me the "get out of the car look" and said: 'Moot,

we know about you and your nosey attorney Quinn too and you ain't getting shit out of my barracks. Now get your god-damn sorry ass out of here.' With that he turned around and started walking back to his office and I yelled out, "Num nuts, I'll be back with a Court Order." Now this is the interesting part, he says: 'You're in way over your head Moot. Get the fuck out of here before I throw you out. I told you, you ain't ever going to see it and a Court Order ain't going to do you no good."

"What'd you say?"

Moot said: "I yelled back: 'That's a double negative.'"

"That was cleaver."

"I thought so."

I said: "The Records Act requires he produce it."

Moot said: "He knows that. I'll tell you, I had the impression he had the Records Act trumped, but I don't know how."

We pulled into the Courthouse garage and made our way through the Courthouse security manned by the usual under trained overweight gun toting Sheriff's deputies. With the State Police force handling crime in rural areas, Sheriff's have been creative in expanding their kingdom the only way possible: Courthouse security. We caught the elevator to the fourth floor to the DA's office, which still had all the original dark oak eloquence of a century old Courthouse. A DA then had the same vision one has now: how long before an opening on the bench so I can get the hell out of petty crime, DUI's, rapes, traffic and murder and run for judge. Every case was viewed with the same paranoia and hope: is this case going to catapult or hinder his chance to wear the black robe? Moot and I waited in the hallway, swapping fish recipes, watching the disheveled public defenders, the guns and blue jeans probation officers, municipal police adorned with their own array of firearms, and defendants with their tattooed families.

After a few minutes the DA secretary came out and escorted us to his office. The sign on his door read Otis "Zero" Nageli, called locally simply "Zero". Moot told me later that he got his nickname from his Catholic high school basketball days.

Otis was a popular happy-go-hunting eighth man on a not so

impressive varsity basketball team. With only four games left in the season, a bored sportswriter for the Tribune Review did a small sports article on how Otis had appeared in nearly every game the last two years and had never scored a point. The writer sarcastically noted that the dismal season was not a complete loss as it had to be a state record to play that much and not score. Otis's coach did not want that moniker, and started Otis full time with instructions to the rest of the team to get him the ball. And for him to shoot.

Otis played hard, as usual, but with one game left he still had not scored. The sports page headline for the final game read "Zero goes for the record tonight!" High school boys and girls, being as they are, wanting a record and having fun at his expense, started to cheer "Zero, Zero" when he missed each attempt. With only a few seconds left, he was fouled and went to the line, shooting two. The first shot rimed out to the crowd's mantra chant of "Zero, Zero Zero." He got the ball back for the second, paused and turned his head to his coach, who had made him play all those minutes. Zero smiled. Behind the coaching bench, to Otis's left, hung an old basketball hoop from the 1943 State Champion's Team, it was the last year the high school had a state record. Otis bounced the ball a few times, then wheeled to his left and faced "Old 43". The crowd went silent. He stared then launched a perfect set shot, catching nothing but net as it went through "Old 43"'s rim. He had scored, and still had the record, much to the chagrin of his coach and delight of his adoring fans. The kids raced on to the floor, put "Zero" on their shoulders, carrying him around, all the while chanting, "Zero, Zero, Zero."

Zero got up from his cluttered desk to greet us, dressed in white rumbled oxford shirt, sleeves rolled up, tie loose. Medium height, bit of a gut, showing a forty's face, mostly bald, but no confidence gap needing a hair sweep across the top. After some quick pleasantries he turned to me and said, enthusiastically:

"Check this out."

He handed me a memo from the American Civil Liberties Union out of Pittsburgh, circulated to the District Attorneys. The memo warned that prosecutions under two new statutes passed by the Pennsylvania legislature would result immediately in a civil rights action if enforced. 9/11 was the green light for law enforcement to get passed police sponsored bills that had been dead lettered in the General Assembly for years. The first was "school" oriented and defined entering a school building with "any chemical that caused death or bodily harm" as a weapon of mass destruction. The second allowed police to monitor your cell phone without a warrant if at a traffic stop. Included was federal funding for devices to intercept cell phone calls within one hundred yards of a police car.

After I glanced through it, and handed it to Moot, Zero said: "What do you think?"

I said: "Sounds like Liquid Plummer is now WMD and the Pennsylvania state police can do what the FBI is prohibited from doing."

"Exactly. Exactly. When they elected the old Zero here, they thought I was the perfect rubber stamp for this entire Robo cop over kill crap they want to pull. I don't give a shit about being reelected but I do give a good god damn about personal freedom."

He slipped down in his chair and stared past us. Almost in a daze. I was about to say something when Zero started again:

"Moot. Quinn. I knew you were coming here before you did. Do you want to know how?"

We both said: "Sure."

"I got a call from Thomas Corbett, Jr."

I said, quizzically: "The United States Attorney out of Pittsburgh?"

"The one and only. You know what he said to me?"

I didn't answer this time and waited.

"He said that he figured you Quinn, and Moot also, would be contacting me to try to get some information about an automobile accident around here in the last couple days. He told me this was now a federal matter and that I should inform you two birds that you could be interfering with a federal investigation. And I, not knowing what he was fucking talking about, but letting him think I did, because I hate the arrogant asshole, said: is that so, under what authority? He said, smooth as conspiracy silk: 'Zero, all I can tell you is that this is from the FBI and Homeland Security.' Now I'm thinking, I don't know of any investigation of any kind and I sure as shit have not seen anything from Homeland Security. So I just feed him a line of crap about respecting jurisdictions, cooperation, how's the office, blah, blah, blah, hang up and start making some calls. The sheriff, the local police, the state police. Nobody knows anything, except an old Statie I know who says for me to check out Bert Tad's obituary."

Zero got up from his chair, now more animated. "I knew Tad. Great old guy. Spent a few hours with him and his wife, Sue, when I was campaigning. So I call the coroner. Ask him what he knows. Says he had the body for about two hours, did a cursory exam, was thinking about an autopsy, when a federal agent, not sure which agency, showed up with an order from somewhere taking custody of the body. The coroner didn't think anything of it, except when they came to get the body, about ten minutes later, a whole fucking fleet of federal cars pulled in. All the Sesame Street size big FBI, DEA and HLS initials slapped all over their blue nylon bowling jackets."

He stopped and looked at us. I said: "It makes sense. We are here to talk about Tad. Moot couldn't get a report on the accident from the State Police."

"Well, Zero owes no one anything but some people owe me some favors, inside and outside the state police. This is going to get personal. The fucking feds thinking they can come in here and tell us here in Westmoreland County what we can and cannot do. I don't represent the police. I represent the people, as trite as that may sound. This doesn't pass the smell test for me. Maybe there's nothing here, but I'm going to find out."

The intercom buzzed, he picked up his phone, listened and said: "Ok. I'll be right down."

Turning to us: "Guys, Judge Cominski has a hair up his ass about a trial tomorrow. Demands my presence. I got to go. Here's my private cell line. Keep in touch."

Handing me a card, he got up, grabbed his jacket, shook our hands and we walked down to the elevator with him. He got off at Three and we proceeded down and out to our car.

When Moot got in the car, he said: "Now what?"

"I don't know. But what bothered you the most about that conversation, if you call it that?"

Moot looked out the window and said: "How the feds knew we were coming down to see Zero."

"Precisely. My guess is they don't like us poking around but aren't sure what we know. Maybe hoping we'll bump into something for them. We'll see how it plays out. Let'm chase us. Hope they're not thinking what an old Sheriff used to say to me when he hauled my clients off to jail."

"What's that?"

"I hope he makes bail. I love it when they run."

Chapter Nineteen

O n the way back from Greensburg, Moot seemed oddly pleased with the role reversal. In his memorable career he was the one pursuing, hiding, trailing, tagging and shadowing others and he found it amusing that he now was being tailed. Whoever they were, they were not particularly discreet, nor threatening, just blatantly blocking access to information.

Moot dropped me at my office and we discussed reloading and getting together maybe later in the week. When I walked in the office, Eva was walking out, telling me there were two messages on my desk and a package delivered by a young man who would not give his name, simply to make sure I got the package. I wished her a pleasant evening. She said it would be as she had a date with a slow walking, good looking, fast taking man.

The first message was from Dean who was at the Pompano Beach office. I punched in the number. Dean answered: "Hello."

"It's Jake, Dean. You called."

"How you doing Jake?"

"Good Dean. What's up?"

"Good. Good." Then a long pause. The mental pump being primed. I waited, then: "Hey, Jake. Alex wanted me to call to tell you that they found his boat."

"That's interesting. Where at?"

"He's not sure, but he heard not too deep. Thinks they can bring it up."

"Any bodies?"

"Don't know. Jake, Alex thinks you ought to come down and check it out."

"I don't know Dean. Tell Alex I'll be down when you get some confirmation on getting it up to the surface."

"I don't think he's going to like that response."

"He'll get over it."

"Ok."

Just as I was hanging up he said: "One more thing. You should know our accountant got a call from his buddy who is an IRS agent out of the Butler office. Wanted to warn us that he thinks we're selected for an audit again."

"Didn't you just go through those two years ago?"

"I know. Trina's going to go postal when she hears that. Why don't you tell her?"

"I'll pass." I avoided talking to Dean about Trina, although it didn't seem to bother him. Nothing seemed to bother Dean. He said: "I hope they have the audit down here. It'd be fun to watch her squirm. See ya Jake."

I looked at the second message: *"Tom Graham wants to talk to you today about Frampton case. Important."*

Calling Graham's number I got his secretary who said he was in a deposition but wanted interrupted. I hit the speaker button, put the receiver down and after a few minutes Graham came on the line: "Quinn. This is Graham."

I wanted to be pissed because he used my last name, but he trumped that by using his own last name. I had no choice but to be pleasant, but really couldn't find it in me, saying: "I figured that out. What do you want?"

"I don't want anything from you Quinn. Marks told me to meet with you. Bring you up to date on our end. You want to meet fine, if not, I'll pass that message along as well."

I thought about it, as Graham already had. Graham knew I wasn't gong to insult Marks, and I knew Marks well enough that he wouldn't ask me to meet with Graham unless he thought it worth my while. I said: "I'll be down tomorrow afternoon."

"Well, that might not fit my schedule."

"Fucking make it fit." I hung up.

I walked around to the other side of my antique mahogany partner's desk and opened the package, which had Tad Industries on the outside, and my name on the label. Inside was a note from Diane on personal stationary and a memo on Tad Industries stationary. Also enclosed was a stamp similar to the one Bryan had showed me, a Bahamian postage stamp, which was raised molded plastic in the face of the former King of England, Edward, the Duke of Windsor. I read her typed note:

Mr. Quinn: This package comes to you by one of our private confidential couriers. I enclose Mr. Tad's dictation to you. I have given you the entire dictation as I think he would want you to have all his thoughts. Please do not contact me. I will call you. ----Diane

The memo was attached and read:

Diane: The next item for dictation is a note to a Mr. Quinn for our meeting. Ten years ago we set up a company on Bimini. Pull that file and put that information on my desk, and rough out this memo to Quinn. I'll think about it tonight, maybe make some calls.

Dear Attorney Quinn:

This letter is to engage your services on behalf of myself and Tad Industries concerning a matter on Bimini. Our request is to keep us informed of all information which directed or tangentially deals with myself or Tad Industries. Neither I nor anyone working on our behalf has any involvement with matters concerning your client Mrs. Frampton, Alex Beck, or affiliated companies. Nor are we currently engaged in any operations in or near Bimini. That is not to say people may be making representations to the contrary and thus the need for your services.

Diane will provide you with the details later and a more formal engagement letter if you require one.

Best regards, Bert Tad.

As much as I wanted to help someone contacting me from the grave, I didn't need cross projects. I put down the letter and stared out the window at the stream of pick-up trucks passing by. I felt the same frustration of trying to get the first answer on a Sunday crossword puzzle. One word and the rest will fall into place. Maybe Frampton's puzzle's starting point was answering the question of who would be interested in Bert Tad's death.

Chapter Twenty

In the morning I successfully moved a stack of files from one side of my desk, then back again, before setting out for Pittsburgh around eleven. Eva told me the Graham meeting was set for two thirty. She also had talked to Bryan and told him I would be coming through, if we could meet, great, if not, for him to call me. I needed to know if he came up with anything else on either of the Frampton's. After the meeting with Graham I hoped to be on the road before rush hour to Washington, D.C. as Eva had been able to get me a meeting with Congressman Taupin. It was time to see just what the people's representative knew.

Pittsburgh traffic was light and I got a spot at the parking garage attached to the Oxford Centre, where Graham's office was located. Several expanding insurance defense firms were located at Oxford, taking three, four or even five floors to house their cadre of young eager associates. How successful, or image conscious, the firm had become was usually determined right out of the gate by the size and décor of the lobby off the elevator. Such lobbies were always manned, so to speak, with a young attractive, by Pittsburgh standards, polite but distant receptionist.

Peters and Marks had seven floors, working on eight. The reception area was the size of my first floor. Cut Italian marble, walled out in dark oak with gold trim paintings of the French and Indian War. The receptionist acted as unpleasantly as the Gucci ad she was trying to replicate. She led me to a conference room just inside the corridor to offices and told me Mr. Graham would be right out. I cynically suspected I wasn't led to his office because he didn't want me to see that he did not have the coveted trifecta corner office with views of the Monongahela, Allegheny and Ohio River.

I leafed through their fresh copy of Architectural Digest and a few minutes later Graham came in, Brooks Brother highly starched white shirt, tie, no jacket, carrying a large multi tabbed file and a cup of coffee. He sat down, saying: "Quinn, Mr. Marks wanted me to meet with you. He's out of the country. He told me to go over some confidential information in the file."

I said: "Ok. Leave the room, give me a few minutes with the file and a copier and I'll be on my way."

He shrugged, and said: "Marks told me to tell you, lawyer to lawyer, that you got none of this from us. We will deny we spoke, so you will have to verify this information through your own sources. If you file interrogatories later and any of this information is requested, well, you can deal with Marks directly then. Agreed?"

What choice did I have? I said, nonchalantly: "Fine. What do you have to tell me?"

He opened the file, pulled out some hand written notes, and a folder, closed the file: "Marks wants you warned about Elizabeth Frampton. We're looking hard at her in the disappearance and death of her alleged husband. We say alleged for now."

From the folder he slid across a copy of Frampton's life insurance policy, which I thumbed through quickly. A standard policy and attached to the back was a copy of the original application. The physician's health form was not attached. He gave me a minute to look through and said: "Obviously it says they were married and when. March 25, 1998, Devon, England. We got a copy of the marriage license from England and it checks out, both signatures. Church ceremony, even registered at the courthouse. But when we checked out the church records, there are none."

"I have to guess that's not going to mean a lot if they have the certificate and both signed. A declaration of marriage is about all they need."

"That's what I said, but they talked to the pastor, who never heard of them." Looking down at his notes again, he continued: "Something else doesn't check out. All her passport records list her marital status as single."

"Ok." I said: "So maybe she didn't update her passport."

"Possible, but it's issued in 2000. And one more thing, her apartment in England has no photos of George Frampton or any other personal items of his."

It was hard to keep the lawyer game face on for that one. She still had a place in England and these guys had illegally searched it? All I did was steal some dirty laundry.

I said: "She probably cleared them out after he died."

"Quinn, he just died. She hasn't left the United States."

I thought back to Moot and I musing about being tailed. I tried to show no reaction and said: "What else?"

"We're trying to contact the physician who confirmed he gave a physical to Frampton." He looked down at his notes, took a drink of his coffee, and then, out of character said: "Hey, you want something to drink?"

I shock my head no and he continued: "You might have guessed that the insurance company's not spending all this effort worrying about a hundred K. We aren't privy to all their files, but there's another policy out there on Frampton"

"How much?"

"Don't know, but my guess, seven figures. It's on the commercial side. We don't have that account but Marks, the Rainmaker, is working on it." He let me absorb that and said: "Finally, Marks got a call from the United States Attorney for Pittsburgh, Tom Corbett. He called Marks as a favor to tell him that there's been a lot of traffic on this case." Closing his file. "That's it."

He got up, walked over to the shredder in the corner and I watched his handwritten notes turn to spaghetti. Melodramatic for my taste. He said: "Do with that what you want, you know the rules under which the information was supplied."

He started to walk out then turned to me and said: "So what do you have on Marks that's he giving you this information?"

I stared back and said: "Friendship's not found in Black's Law Dictionary, you wouldn't understand."

"Fuck you Quinn. We'll see who gets the last snide remark in this case."

He walked out. I followed, past the receptionist, into the

elevator to the ground floor, past a series of silver and neon boutiques with nary a customer ever, except Starbucks. I ordered an ice tea, looking for Bryan who text messaged me to meet there. Eva had reminded him I was on a tight schedule. Surprisingly, Bryan was already at one of the aluminum tables just under the spiral walkway where a baby grand piano used to be. Several years ago the landlord came to the realization that you can't take the 'Burgh out the Pittsburgh and the much talented but unappreciated and unheard tuxedoed piano man was relieved of his lonely duties and the baby grand put in storage. I went over to Bryan's table, which had an assortment of papers laid out on it, and said, before sitting down:

"Bryan, has anyone else contacted you about Frampton?"

"Not really, but I'll get to that later."

As I sat down, he said: "Your boy Frampton has more people hunting for his ideas than a ten-point on opening day."

He smiled at his metaphor, offered for my benefit, as Bryan's only interest in hunting would be calculating the trajectory of the bullet. Bryan continued: "They tell you anything at Corning?"

I kept it short: "Not much, except you might say Frampton and Corning had a falling out."

"Corning has a full court press out there to find out if Frampton is still alive, and if not, where their money and ideas are. Have you been followed lately?"

"I don't know, maybe." I said.

"Well, if you are it's a good chance its iJet because Corning hired them to find out about the Frampton's, and probably you too."

Bryan had used iJet on an immigration file of mine the year before. iJet was the non-covert intelligence envy of the spy world. Based in Annapolis Maryland, these former NSA spooks supply real-time foreign intelligence to private business and high-end travelers. They were the premiere private international investigative agency whose reputation solidified in 2001. Seven top executives of Global Forecast, a hedge mutual fund, did not show for work at floor eighty-nine of the South Tower of the World Trade Center on the morning of September 11. The rumor, still not confirmed, was that the no-show was based upon information supplied as a client of iJet.

"Interesting. Can't say I'm good at knowing if I'm being followed, but I guess I should start." I said.

Leaning back in my chair, starting to crystallize some thoughts, I glanced at my watch and realized I needed to get going. Bryan had a file on the table with the letters DARPA on the tab. I pointed at the file as I got up to throw my tea away.

Bryan said: "It's just an article about DARPA."

"Which is?"

"The Defense Advanced Research Projects Agency. You never heard about those guys?"

I shook my head no.

"Right out of the Pentagon, but not in their budget. The liberal's idea. As long as most of the money goes to professors and university start-ups, they think it's great. Military research that has to be linked to defense, not offensive weapons. Sometimes their contracts are open bid, available to the public. Since 9/11, anyone with an idea linked to terrorism is given a shot at some of those sweet no-strings, no accounting government money. I put the article in because I know Corning has had a lot of DARPA money in the last few years. In fact, their positive cash flow depends on it."

"When I met them they said the government was on their case about Frampton and a palm pilot. You think it is DARPA?" I said.

"Could be."

I checked my watch. "Bryan, I have to get going to beat the traffic."

He got up and we walked though the lobby to the parking garage elevators. On the way he said: "One more thing. Last time I ran Frampton up and down the internet, our "tracer" program popped up saying someone was trying to get inside our computer."

"Tracer?' I said.

"Since we occasionally, inadvertently" said with a wry smile "get into someone else's computer, we developed software to let us know if we're being followed. Sure enough, every time we poked around looking for Frampton material, a "tracer" trailed us back to try to get inside our computer. We've blocked it so far, but this is powerful clever stuff and they're going to crack in soon."

"So who's following you?"

"I don't know. Which puzzles me. It's not a private firm as I can trace that quickly, even iJet. It's not the FBI, because that's easy to trace back to forensics in West Virginia. We call it "Byrd Shit", in honor of the great white topped Senator. So then you have the CIA, but they're like the reverse of the FBI. They can't get a domestic tap without FBI approval, so they violate your rights by sending their tap in from overseas. This is domestic. It has to be the latest equipment and coming I think from just outside of the D.C. area. I'll let you know if we figure it out."

I nodded. "Get the tattoo, yet?"

"Still researching. One more thing. In that DARPA folder I put in an article one of the guys over at FreeMarkets mentioned to me yesterday. It's about investing in start up companies and some that might soon be publicly traded. Ovonics is one of the areas and Frampton's mentioned twice. I'm still working on the Wall Street angle."

He walked with me to the garage telling me he would let me know if he found anything out. I drove my car down Grant Street, to Route 22, through the Squirrel Hill tunnels to the Turnpike. Just past getting my ticket at the booth entrance for the Turnpike and passing under the sign "Harrisburg, Washington, D.C. East" my cell phone rang. The caller i.d. was "unknown number." I answered: "Hello, Quinn."

"Attorney Quinn. This is Diane, Mr. Tad's secretary. I see you're just getting on the Turnpike. Call me in an hour and I'll tell you where we can meet."

Puzzled, looking around and seeing no cars, no overpasses, I said: "Well, I'm on my way out of town. And…"

She interrupted: "Don't tell me Mr. Quinn. I'll find you and tell you where to meet. I'll see you in an hour or two. Ok?"

"Ok." I said, thinking I must need to be told what to do by women. Women every which way messing with my mind. Too much stuff.

Chapter Twenty-One

——

An hour and half east on I-76, known to Pennsylvanian's simply as The Turnpike, Diane called my cell asking me to get off at the next exit, Route 30 East toward Chambersburg. I wanted to discuss that unilateral decision, but I had to stay overnight somewhere, as my meeting in D.C. was not until the next day, so without protest I traced General Robert E. Lee's route to Gettysburg. A few miles outside of Gettysburg she called again, this time telling me to meet her at Devil's Den Micro Brewery on Fifth Street.

I parked down the street from the Devil's Den Micro, not noticing anyone following me, but thinking if they were good at what they did, I wouldn't. The Brewery was located inside one of several civil war era brick buildings on a side alley. A small set of cooper brewery tank in a glass enclosure was just off the entrance. I obeyed the Seat Yourself command and took a booth. The bartender, dressed in Civil War attire, trudged over acting as if he was forced to play the part of a Sergeant, while waiting for a bigger role, one that fit his skills, maybe a Colonel or General. He described the beers and recommended either *Reynold's Shadow,* for the revered Pennsylvania General killed on the first day, or *The Devil to Pay,* after Col. John Buford's defense of Seminary Ridge. I said either was fine and while he went to pour me a tin mucket, the civil war canteen, I perused the memorabilia on the walls and wondered why Diane just didn't tell me from the beginning to meet her here.

Sarge brought me a dark wheat *Devil To Pay* as Diane walked in, alone, large purse, casual outfit, greeting smile that kind of defensive smile women use when entering a safe but not familiar room. I walked over, we shook hands, and I led her to my window booth. She was an attractive full-figured, as they say, woman, and she carried herself well, that image of "yeah, I could be a little thinner, but I'm not, and, you know what, I'm pretty comfortable with myself." She reminded me of a woman who wouldn't mind being taken care of, but she has had to go it alone and settled into that comfort. She looked different than when we last met, so I took a chance men rarely should and commented on her hair, which was shorter with a lighter tint of blond:

"Did you get your hair cut? *It* looks nice that way." Avoiding the more personal, "You".

"Thanks. I got it cut yesterday. Needed a change. Maybe Mr. Tad's death had me on edge, but I should have done it long ago."

The Sergeant brought Diane a mucket without asking, to which I said: "Been here before?"

"Few times."

"What's with the cloak and dagger getting here? And following me, always knowing where I was?"

"Mr. Quinn, if you don't know by now, Tad Industries is not what you think. We have access to technology the public will never see. Your cell phone for us is a homing beacon. I didn't give directions because I had to make sure you weren't being followed."

"Am I?"

"For now, no."

She took a rather dainty sip from her silver muckett, put it down and pulled from her purse a small three ring binder, Tad Industries and Confidential printed on the front. The binder in front of her, she folded her hands over it, squared her head, making sure of eye contact, any softness in her face gone: "Before we get to why I asked to meet, I want to tell you about my relationship with Mr. Tad."

I said, probably without thinking, a trait I perfected with women: "That's not necessary, it's none of my business."

"I'm not telling for you, I'm telling for me. I want to hear it myself. And maybe someone else should know, even if it's one person. You're the chosen one, I guess, like or not."

With that she continued: "I attended a college down the road from Ligonier, St. Vincent's. It was as close to a convent my dad could find." That said with a smile. "My second college summer I got a job working at Tad's stables, cutting grass, working horses, driving Susan here and there. Loved it. The next summer they moved me inside to the office doing odds and ends, mainly filing, answering the phone on occasion. It was a small office at the house. You've been there."

She took a drink, while I nodded about having seen the office.

"Computers were just coming into use then and I had some knowledge because then the universities were ahead of the curve. So I helped upgrade the office and it was fun. Then Mr. Tad had me work on the Coke deal. He had a contact in Atlanta with Coke, got the Coke franchise for plastic memorabilia and we needed a manufacturer in Hong Kong. I flew overseas with him, and, if I remember right, with his brother Andrew too, who has since died. Around that same time I was dating a student at St. Vincent, and, surprise, I got pregnant. Although he said he would marry me, it was more obligation than love. I said no. He was killed in a car wreck about a month before my baby boy was born."

She reached into her purse, pulled out her wallet, and got a picture of a young man in his early twenties wearing a Navy uniform. "That's my son Michael with me when he graduated from the Naval Academy."

As she was putting Michael back, our Sergeant came by and we both ordered the soup, and another mucket. I had switched to *Reynolds* in honor of the 84th Pennsylvanians who saved Little Round Top, nary a mention by Professor Chamberlain. She said: "When Michael was born there were some vicious rumors about Mr. Tad and me, one that put a strain on his marriage, and his Rolling Rock social world. I kept my silence as to real father, which probably was a mistake, but I knew the father's parents and I wanted my child to have nothing to do with them, which reflected the wishes of the father as well. He had escaped their abuse. I confided this with Mr. Tad, who stood by me in my decision and although I offered to resign, he would have none of that. It was not even as if it was our little secret. No ulterior motive. I think it became a matter of principle for him. I dropped out of St. Vincent, stayed on with Tad Industries. Over the years Mr. Tad endured the snide remarks on occasion, as did I. But we knew the truth. The truth is he never made a pass at me once, never even a hint of it."

She paused and there was an awkward silence and the beginning of what I thought might be tears. But there were none.

"I related all this to you so you understand my loyalty to Mr. Tad."

I felt no need to respond, simply a nod, recognition. She opened the binder, looked down and then up to me and said, plainly, unemotionally: "I have serious questions whether Mr. Tad's death was accidental. Let's start with the autopsy."

She pulled the first several pages out of the binder and slid them across the table to me. Stamped across the right corner in red was: *H.L.S.: Confidential.*

I said: "We were told there was no autopsy."

Her stoic expression did not change.

"Mr. Quinn. Do not take offense, try all you might, you do not have access to the same information that Tad Industries has."

She took another drink, this time a rather long slow one, one that revealed some Western PA local bar heritage. As I started to read, she said:

"You'll find two reports there. The first is the one the public might see: blunt force trauma to the head, subdural hematoma the actual term. Head hit the windshield. But flip over to the second page, the one marked HS/IS. That stands for Homeland Security-Internal/Security. That report is for the eyes of the Director, his direct staff and their Internal Security Team. We don't know a lot about that team, and in fact no one knows a lot about the agency, except what they want us to know: kindergarten warning colors. Our ex-governor Tom Ridge has controlled the agency and even Congress doesn't know what they're up to. And doesn't want to. The less they know the better for them. Plausible deniability."

She reached in her purse and pulled out a pack of cigarettes. She didn't open the pack, setting them beside her. "You'll see that the head injury was there, but probably wasn't enough to kill him. Not conclusive, but it's suggested that he suffocated. Fabric particles inside of his mouth, captured on the magnified pictures on page three. Homeland marks this as potential homicide, then "Request Director approval for further investigation."

"What does Homeland Security have in this?"

"We're not sure. We know that Homeland does not have any authority to investigate anything on their own, unless it involves a potential threat to national security. Otherwise, they just refer it to the FBI, DEA, etc."

"So what's your guess?"

"Well, all this started after you called and visited our office asking questions about Cat Cay."

She let that float in the air. If she was looking for a response she didn't get one. She said: "I want to tell you some things about Mr. Tad and Tad Industries. And to do that Mr. Quinn I need your trust. And I don't know about that yet. Mr. Tad and I had you checked out and we thought you were ok. We intended on discussing retaining you for the company."

She reached into her purse. Women have at least one of three accessory fetishes: shoes, jewelry, or purses. Hers must be purses and large ones, as it seemed a bottomless pit. She pulled out an envelope, leaned it sideways against my mucket and said:

"Inside you will find twenty-five thousand dollars in cash."

She noticed the look on my face which was somewhere between offended and curious.

"What do you buy for this?" I asked with a slight edge to my voice, not looking inside the envelope, just moving it to the side, away from the sweat of my beer, but not any closer to Diane.

She opened the pack of cigarettes, the narrow Capry Lights, picked up the lighter, and with the cigarette already at her lips and ready to flick the lighter, said: "Mind if I smoke?"

"No. Go right ahead."

"Thanks. I'm trying to start." Said with a coy smile.

Awkwardly fumbling with her cigarette, making me think she really was trying to start, she said: "Well, Jake. You don't mind if I call you Jake, do you?"

"No, I'd prefer that, should have told you that earlier, but didn't know what distance you wanted to keep."

Interrupting she said: "Really? You don't know much about women do you Jake?"

"What?" I said somewhat surprised at the sudden shift to a more personal level combined with a nugget of truth.

"Forget I said that. Look, the cash is not for legal advice, or a legal retainer. The cash is mine alone, not through Tad Industries. I want you to help me and I don't want you worrying about expenses or cost. I could give you a credit card, but Mr. Tad and I found over the years that hundred dollar bills, not tens and twenties, open doors and enhance people's memory. Trust me on this: none of these bills are traceable and all are legal tender."

I decided to wait to make a decision on taking the money, saying: "Right now my plates pretty full just figuring out my client's insurance claim that lead me to your office. I don't need to be worried about a conflict in whom I represent."

She could see I was about to push the envelope back to her side of the table when Sarge came with our soup. I had to pick up the envelope and move it even closer to me. We stopped talking, as people do when a waiter comes by. She said: "If you think you get to a position that violates your standards just let me know and you're out. Keep the balance of the cash. But I have information that will get you much further along and much quicker, all to the benefit of your client."

"I'm listening."

She put out her quarter smoked cigarette. She said: "Have you ever heard of In-Q-Tel, Jake?"

I shook in the negative.

"Not many people have. But it's not a complete secret. In-Q-Tel is the CIA's venture capital arm. Tech companies were zooming ahead on breakthroughs for business but the CIA's needs are different, as you can imagine. Instead of hiring inside, they fund companies, starting some, to develop technology they need for U.S. security operations."

She lit another cigarette. "They funded Language Weaver.

Makes software development for Arabic translation, which is harder than you think. Let's see. Keyhole which developed a massive data base for satellite images. And then there's Nanosys."

She paused, I think to see if I had a reaction, which I didn't. I said: "What do they do?"

"They do what the name implies. Develop nanotechnology systems."

I said, getting the point now: "Like George Frampton was working on?"

"Right."

"Tad was in with Alex or Frampton on nanotech stuff?" I said, surprised tone not disguised.

"No. Not at all. We've had a number of CIA contracts over the years. Mostly legitimate businesses that helped sponsor or cover some CIA operatives. A lot of Bahama activity, not terrorism tracking, more keeping track of Cuba. And that often leads to some cross over with Drug Enforcement."

I said, thinking about what Bryan had told me: "What about DARPA?"

She said with a disgusted tone: "Those Defense guys are a pain in the ass. That's all military industrial, all large corporate cocktail crap."

"So what's the scuba diving operation where Tad's name came up have to do with this?"

"That's what we don't know either. We have a stake in Nanosys, but really just funneling the CIA money. The old scuba shop had nothing to do with that. Remember when Mr. Tad brought me into your meeting?"

I nodded affirmatively.

"That was no act that he didn't know anything. Simply put: someone was using our name from before. And that's what Mr. Tad started asking around about after you left that day."

"Did Alex know about your involvement in Nanosys?"

"Yes. But not much. Simply a passing comment to Alex by Mr. Tad several months ago. You need to know that Mr. Tad and Alex go back a long way. Mr. Tad was a member of the Cat Cay club before Alex showed up. In fact, Mr. Tad sponsored

Alex and his family to get in."

She paused, trying to relight the cigarette, fumbling again with the lighter, so this time I took the lighter and helped, she saying: "You know, I should quit, but I'm no quitter. I'm going to lick this and get started smoking."

She continued: "I can also tell you this. After you left, he called Tom Ridge directly. Here's the interesting part: Ridge doesn't confirm or deny any Homeland involvement. And he assured Bert, which is what Tom called him, that he would find out what it was all about."

We stared at each other. I glanced at the autopsy report again. She said: "I'll make this blunt and easy. A man you know, just briefly, was killed. You feel connected with him. Logic tells you that it was not your fault that you're not involved. But there is an undeniable emotional component. Even without me asking, you're already thinking about finding who did this. You don't think Alex was involved. If you're right, use the money to save him, his precious daughter, yourself, I don't care who, just find out who did this."

When she stopped talking she took a drag on the cigarette, this time as if she had been smoking all her life, making me wonder if everything was an act. I stared at her for the longest time, then took the envelope and put it in my back pocket.

I said: "Why not just hire someone in the business. Some covert operative or a detective agency."

"Because at this point we don't know who to trust. We want a fresh face."

Fresh or naïve? I thought to myself.

"How do I get a hold of you?" I said.

"I'll find you. If you call me don't be explicit. You never know whose listening. And one more thing. I have a friend making some inquiries around Washington, if he comes up with anything I'll let you know."

She started returning everything to her purse. She stood up and said, softly: "Hey, thanks for listening."

We both got out of the booth, Diane picking up the check, which I tried to grab unsuccessfully.

I said: "Diane, so is the twenty five really yours?"

She moved very close to me, pressing her body against my side, and said quietly: "Two days ago I got a call from S&T Bank's trust department. Unknown to me, Mr. Tad had set up a trust fund for me some time ago. They tell me the fund's worth more than twenty million dollars. I tell you that because no matter what it takes, no matter how much money, I want you to figure this out and find out who did this."

She paused and softly added: "I also tell you that so if you need a date with a very wealthy woman, give me a call. You know I know how to find *you*."

She pulled back and I couldn't help but smiling. We were out the door and walking toward her car when she said she was probably heading back to Ligonier that night and if she got tired she would get a motel room. I really didn't take it as any type of offer for me to join her and I'm not sure what I would have done had it been one. As she was getting in her car, I stopped her and pulled out the envelope and handed it back to her, saying: "Diane, I'll bill you."

"I didn't think you'd take it. Tonight, anyway."

She reached in her purse, pulled her hand out and said: "Here. If you show this to right people, they may be able to help you."

It was a plastic raised Bahaman stamp of the Duke of Windsor.

"Who do I show it to?"

"You'll figure it out if you have to. Be careful out there."

She drove off. I waited at the street to see if anyone was following her. As I walked to my car, I felt a chill and maybe a faint sound in the distance, hoping someone was sending me an angel and it wasn't the devil knocking at my door.

Chapter Twenty-Two

I spent the night outside of Washington and drove in early, full rush hour, for my meeting with Congressman Richard Taupin. People proclaim the need for "life in the open, life in the country", but the giant housing glacier engulfing Maryland and Virginia from the epicenter of D.C. seemed evidence to the contrary. I paid quick respects to Washington, Lincoln and Jefferson as I came off the Parkway and Key Bridge, finding a lucky break Mall side parking near the Rayburn Office building.

No longer walking "undetected" into the Capitol or Congressional offices, I passed through a cadre of metal detectors and security personnel at all entries and exits. Once inside I made my way to Taupin's office, close access to the Capitol, reflecting his pecking order in "doing the people's business". Outside his door were listed his Committee positions: Chair: Homeland Security; Vice Chair: Subcommittee on Coal, Oil and Natural Resources; Member: Ways and Means, Social Security, Transportation and Defense.

Entering his office I was greeted by his young, pretty, smiling receptionist. She asked my name, confirmed that I had an appointment and I was told Helen would be out in a minute. Sitting down on the leather couch, I surveyed the dark mahogany walls, rich green carpet. The walls held an array of constituent "meet and greet" photos, interspersed with the Congressman and the President: Oval Office, Camp David and one that appeared to be at a military base. Jealous thoughts ran through my mind, as I pictured Trina waiting on the same couch, then leaving with her Congressman for an afternoon at the Willard.

Within a minute Helen, a pushing forty, no nonsense business suited lady, came through a door to the left of the receptionist desk. I thought I recognized her from a function I attended in Pennsylvania, but wasn't sure. Politicians rarely let their two worlds collide. The female staff at a state capital or Washington, D.C. rarely visits the front lines. They are typically stylish urban and their condescending attitude, no matter how disguised, will eventually be exposed on the home front. A sign of non-humility is fatal to an elected public servant.

Helen, pleasant but formal, led me into the Congressman's personal office, through yet another door. Congressman Richard Taupin was sitting behind his desk, phone in hand, crisp white shirt and tie, with sleeves slightly rolled up. Didn't look any older than the last time I saw him. Women hate to love his breed, but can't help themselves. He pointed to me to have a seat, indicating he would be off in a minute. A pro, he mentioned no names in my presence and he made no attempt to impress me by suggesting he was digesting a world issue, or just ordering lunch. He gave simple answers to whoever he was speaking with: yes, no, maybe, ok, and finally: "Call Helen, she'll set something up when I get back, I'll see what I can do. No promises."

He hung up, quickly rose, came over to where I was gawking at pictures on the walls, and greeted me with: "Jake, good to see you." Then gesturing to the couch, said: "Have a seat. Have a seat." Mocking himself in almost a bad southern accent said: "Damn good to see a fine, fine member of my constituency down here in Washington. Keeps me honest. Keeps me honest. Quinn, now is that spelled with one "e" or two?"

He paused as I smiled and he said: "How was that? Sincere enough?"

"Yes, indeed."

"Really, no shit Jake, it's good to see you."

"Well, I appreciate you seeing me Congressman. I know you're busy."

We exchanged some pleasantries about mutual acquaintances, a few "what's this one up to" or that one, then he said, seriously: "Jake, I got to tell you, I got your message and what you wanted to talk about. I had one of the eager beavers here try to get you some usable information."

There was a slight inflexion with the word "usable". I said: "Congressman, I hope you know that if it was just a case, just legal, I wouldn't bother you, but I think the information I need only the government has access to."

"I know. You want to know whether Alex and Trina are on someone's radar screen here at spook central. Jake", using my first name repeatedly, "information is power in this town. When you seek information and someone gives it up, even if it's their job, you have to pay back that borrowed power. But with Trina, and Alex too, I tried to get as much as I'm allowed to know."

He got up from his seat, walking and talking, starting a speech that seemed ready made for a Rotary Club: "Jake, we're on a history time quest in this country. We're a smart, resourceful, but not patient, people. This is our century, maybe even centuries. The Ottoman, Greek, Roman, even English Empires, had their time. The smart asses here in Washington think we're different. More humane. More just. More benevolent. More tolerant. But historians don't think so. They say we are just like those before us. Civilization is not a continuum. It has slipped away before and it can happen again."

"Jake, I believe this. There are parts of this world that are unworthy of our respect and mercy. They're evil. Pure and simple. And they've brought that to our shores, and if we are to continue as a civilized society they need eradicated. It's like this: a doctor will tell you, you're not cancer free so long as one cancer cell is still in your body. You're not free until they are all destroyed. And even then you have to go back and keep checking."

The intensity in his voice had calmness as well. He was one of the many that viewed 9/11 as a crossroads. I just wondered what the hell I was getting this speech for. What the hell did any of this have to do with me or my requests? I wanted to interject that Hitler made the same argument when he invaded Russia: free the world of communism for western civilization.

But, he was not done. Seemed to be just warming up. He continued: "You know when you can tell an issue is complicated? When the NRA and ACLU are arguing the same side. Jake, it's a balancing act. Everyday a group is in here.

Half want all the foreigners deported, except the ones of course changing their kid's diapers or mowing their country clubs. The other half wants us to make all the aliens legal, except of course the bad guys who hijack planes, and we should know the difference. They want the FBI to do more, but the CIA less. Or is it the other way around? And everyone has 20/20 hindsight. You're either with us or against us, Jake."

I didn't know if he wanted an answer, but it seemed like he did. I decided just to stare back. Not defiantly, just recognition that I was hoping it was a rhetorical question. After a few seconds, he started looking out the windows, then at a picture on his wall of the aftermath of the Pentagon on 9/11, finally hitting his intercom and saying: "Send in Kilmare."

Evan Kilmare, as he was introduced to me, came through a wall rather than a door, like that goofy door in the Oval Office of the White House that looks like a wall. Kilmare epitomized what I distained in a politician's staff: young, good looking, J-Crew all the way, a swagger that I would love to see him try to pull off at Murdock's Bar and Grill. And smooth. It was hard to dislike someone that smooth. I ignored all the usual pleasantries, acting as childish as possible. Helen walked in and said: "Congressman, you have a vote in ten minutes." Taupin, grabbing his jacket, rolling down his sleeves, said:

"Jake, I have to go." Giving Kilmare a look. "Evan will give you everything we have. Good seeing you."

Kilmare squinting at me, then looking at the Congressman, said: "Sir. I don't think we can do that, without you being present. He has no clearance at all."

Taupin glared at Kilmare as Helen handed Taupin a note. He said to Helen, intending it also to Kilmare, disturbed: "Issue him god damn level 5 clearances under my signature for today. See you later Jake. Good luck."

He shook my hand and was out, choosing door No. 1. There was nothing behind it.

Kilmare put his briefcase on the desk, making a circus act out of the combinations to open. Well thought out security precaution, unless I chose simply to steal the whole fucking case and run out the door. Pulling out a file, he took off the tied red string and said: "Congressman Taupin had me ask around the agencies about your clients. See if there are any government shenanigans. I'll start with Alex", showing a familiarity with his first name that came only from actual acquaintance.

He said: "He's showing up on a number of reports with the Securities Commission, information that you could get digging around yourself at the SEC, if you knew what you were looking for."

I showed no reaction to the snide condescending comment.

"Alex has a company that has filed through Morgan Stanley's branch in Pittsburgh for a stock offering involving some high end tech gadgets. Maybe you knew this, maybe you didn't, but George Frampton is listed as a principal or at least has enough interest to require his name to be on the filing. The offering's been delayed twice, nothing unusual there but the SEC has had so many inquiries from Corning and government agencies that it's starting to issue letters of inquiry to Morgan Stanley."

He leafed though some papers, continuing: "The inside information is that Corning wants it stopped. They suggest that Frampton stole proprietary information via the government and that it is protected. I mean really protected. Level 6 information that even I cannot get to."

That last phrase was just to let me know how high up this information must be. My guess was that it was at the Calvin Klein level, as opposed to lowly level 5- JCrew.

I said: "So who are the people following me? Our government?"

"Who knows?"

There was a long pause as he put most of the file back in the briefcase, the conclusion being that this meeting was over. I said: "Anything else."

"Just one more. Congressman Taupin wanted you to see this. It's a note he received from his liaison at the Pentagon. He told me to have you read it, and then destroy it."

He handed me a sheet with a type written note. Thinking the whole thing over the top, I read the note:

Congressman: On the matter we discussed, to our knowledge none of the government resources are deployed investigating any of these matters. Appropriate calls have been made to the insurance carrier and your constituents should find their claims being settled shortly so they can move on.

Kilmare snatched the paper from me and said: "The Congressman hopes this helps you. I have to go Mr. Quinn. Lunch with Congresswoman Grube's new paralegal. Over at Georgetown. Helen will show you to the door."

Kilmare put the note in the shredder, leaving as Helen came in escorting me to the door, hoping I had a nice day. Walking to my car, it started to impact me just how out of control this whole little case had become. Any lawyer will tell you a bad case with a good client, is better than a good case with a bad client. I didn't know which was which at this point. But it was dawning on me how deep I was in over my head. I thought how easy it was for them to look you in the eyes and tell you sweet lies.

Chapter Twenty-Three

—

Passing through Dulles International's art deco dome uneventfully, I rushed to catch a two-thirty direct to Miami. Oblivious to the crowd, I fixated on the note Kilmare had supplied in the morning. What possible interest would the government have in seeing Elizabeth Frampton settle her insurance claim? Unless, which I suspected, Alex had made a call to Taupin and asked for pressure. Would Alex tell if he had? I doubt it. And Taupin was disturbingly silent about any meeting with Trina. Was that analysis on my part, or jealousy? But that didn't confront me none. I was jealous of everything.

Trying to collect my thoughts on the plane ride down proved futile, so I spent it engaged in conversation with the passenger beside me. Whatever your troubles, how can you pass on talking to an eighty year old Jewish diamond merchant who knew Bugsy Segal and Meyer Lansky personally? I learned the hit on Bugsy had nothing to do with the Las Vegas Flamingo, but was contracted by his girlfriend. Not that the mob was upset with his passing. Marylyn Monroe was a sweetheart, and Kennedy was an ass. And Frank Sinatra was underrated. Told me to listen to Frank's version of "Lady is a Tramp" and compare it to any song, before or after. On a whim, I asked him if he ever heard of Bert Tad. He said no. I felt relieved knowing at least one person wasn't involved in Frampton's case.

Off the plane, I made my way easily through the massively sterile continuous erector set of the Miami Airport complex and headed to my reserved car at Budget. It's really no cheaper than Hertz, but I don't like being a member of any club, even though they don't seem to have regular meetings. It's the fact that anyone can join. I picked out a Mustang and headed north on I-95 toward Fort Lauderdale, keeping the window down, feeling the thick Florida heat. Eva had arranged a room at the Marriot near the Merritt Boat works where I hoped to get some more information on the status of Alex's sunken boat.

The drive took about an hour and I checked in, threw my stuff in some drawers and decided to go over to Parker's Crab House and Bar, an old haunt from back in the Trina excursion to Florida days. Driving over I considered calling Trina, but didn't. She would start whining about all the government interference in her business and I wasn't in the mood. Besides, she didn't contact me and I was always good at holding my breath in a relationship. It's just so awkward when I pass out.

Parker's hadn't changed in the last twenty years, never would as long as Lou Parker held title. Making money at The Crab House was no longer on Lou's mind, although it still did. His waterfront acre on paper made him a beach block multi-millionaire, so the beer was cheap and the fish still ocean fresh. Like so many restaurateurs, it was in his blood. Where would he go and what would he do if he sold out?

The décor never changed. Clap board walls, nets hung from the ceiling, lobster tank, tables circling an old pine bar. I ordered a Heineken and a bowl of conch chowder. The bartender, Mo, told me Lou was out fishing and would probably be in later. I savored the best of German's bottled beer and the chowder, watching whatever was overhead on the television, thinking that brunettes must have been wiped out by a TV plague, as only blonds and pitch black haired ladies anchored the news.

A blond woman sat down beside me at the bar. A woman I knew, in fact, one that I represented. She put her hand on my shoulder, and said: "What do they say? Fancy meeting you here?"

I tried to disguise that dull stare you get when someone appears you either haven't seen for sometime or you don't expect. Speechless seeing Elizabeth Frampton at my side, my thoughts were: how did she know I was here? After a few seconds, she said: "Well, are you going to buy me a drink?"

I finally stood up, moved the stool beside me out for her and said: "Sure, what would you like?"

"A Manhattan. Lou makes a great Manhattan."

Raising my hand to Mo, who was staring at my blond client, I ordered a Manhattan and another beer for myself. Elizabeth Frampton, quite comfortably, as if this was an arranged meeting, said: "How's my case coming along Attorney Quinn?"

I wanted to say, you know so much, tell me. But I deferred, saying: "Mrs. Frampton, to be honest, I'm not sure." Which was actually being honest.

She nodded, waited as our drinks appeared, and said: "Well, can you bring me up to date? Have you talked to the insurance company lately?"

Sensing she knew something, I went ahead, cautiously: "I know nothing more about your husband's disappearance. I'm down here right now because they found the boat."

"I know. What else? Have you talked to the insurance company, which was my original question?" She said abruptly but with a smile.

"I've talked to the attorney for the carrier and they seem nervous. Why, I don't know."

Her tone caused me to withhold mentioning anything else, particularly the note read to me in Washington. The British were so good at jacketing their emotions. How could two races, the Irish and British, be so geographically close, and yet worlds apart on that score?

She said: "Attorney Quinn. I think you're a fine chap. Probably a good barrister from what they tell me. And an honest one. Probably too honest, if there is such a thing, and life tells me there is. Let me speak plainly. I'm instructing you as my solicitor to call the carrier tomorrow, speak to whoever you need to, and tell them to wire transfer the settlement in full to this account within ten days."

With that pronouncement she handed me one of Alex's personal business cards where she had written on the back a bank account number. Using Alex's card was no random act.

I said: "Mrs. Frampton, trust is a two way street. I don't like being told what to do, and I would appreciate it if you would tell me what you know and why you are setting up this demand now."

121

Grinning saying: "As my solicitor Quinn, you should know that you owe me trust, I only owe you a fee."

Stung, but unfazed, I said: "Well, I can end that right here, right now."

She smiled, that condescending smile women can give men to make them feel like little boys. She said: "Oh, I don't think you will do that."

She had nothing on me and I owed her nothing. My instincts told me to walk away, but disregarding instincts comes naturally to me. Representing her for now kept me in the game. I wanted to know what she knew. Did she know what had been related to me by Taupin?

I played with my bottle for a few seconds, didn't say anything, and she pardoned herself to the washroom. When she came back, I decided it was time to explore another piece of the puzzle. I said:

"I'll call the carrier's lawyer tomorrow." And added: "I hope you know what you're doing, this could go south on you real quick. Let me give you some advice, legal or otherwise. When you get the insurance money, I think your problems are not over. One item that keeps popping up is your husband's palm pilot, and the people looking for it mean business."

She said, not missing a beat: "Quinn, the palm pilot is *my other* insurance policy. And I'm pleased you brought it up. I figured you were looking for it just like everyone else, even my Alex."

She reached into her Chinese Prada and pulled out a silver metal case, slightly bigger than a cigarette pack. Laying it on the bar, she put her palm over it and said:

"As my solicitor I am entrusting this package to you. I'll not jeopardize your credibility with others by telling you what's inside. I don't have to. Fair enough."

I said: "No, that's not fair enough." And began to push it back in her direction on the bar.

"Come on, Jake." Using my first name for the first time. "There are two things that drive you: loyalty and ego. Your ego takes over when someone says you can't do it. Maybe you were bullied in the playground. Maybe you were the bully. Who knows, I don't know your trigger. And you pride yourself now on being loyal and standing up to bullies. You feel yourself weak sometimes, you need help being loyal or standing up, but there's no one to help, so you dig even deeper. Isolate yourself even more. No. You'll take my silver case. My guess is you've already decided that it's a card worth holding, or bait for whoever's chasing you or whoever or whatever you're chasing."

"Dangerous stuff Mrs. Frampton." I said.

"You don't think I've figured out how dangerous all this business is with Alex." She laughed. "Scares me less than the thought of living the rest of my life shopping at Wal-Mart. I'm not naïve about anything. Not at my age. Neither should you be. You're in deep. Holding what's inside that case protects us both. Don't take it and you could get us both killed. And maybe Alex and your Trina too."

"All of this for a one hundred thousand dollar insurance policy?" I said.

"Think what you want, just do your job for me and Alex. And it will all work out and you'll be handsomely paid. Monetarily and otherwise if you prefer." She dropped her hand to my thigh and squeezed it slightly. I moved her hand back to the bar and said: "What if they don't want to settle...."

She cut me off: "They will. Trust me."

"Let me finish. If by chance they don't and we file suit, I have to sign the complaint. I have to certify that I have a reasonable basis to believe the facts are supportable by evidence. Are you going to tell me then what happened to your husband?'

She said: "It won't come to that. But if it did, you have my word: George Frampton is not alive."

I said: "Funny, that doesn't seem very comforting to me."

She started to get up and leave and said: "Don't take the pilot to your whiz kid computer buddy. Only I have the code for what's inside. Punch in the wrong numbers and it's useless, as will your hand be if holding it. Next time we talk, we'll talk about the code. Don't let me down, my life is in the palm of your hand."

As she got up she put her left hand on my shoulder, then as she moved on, her hand went across the back of my neck, scrapping her fingernails into my neck, causing me to grab her hand, with pain obvious in my face. She smiled, a sensuous tempting smile. I let go of her hand. She walked out, but when near the door, turned and said: "Don't forget to get the check."

I checked my neck, slightest trace of blood on my fingers. I had a napkin on my neck as Lou Parker came in. We sat and talked for awhile and I eventually asked Lou if I needed to store something valuable could he help. He said sure. I stayed awhile longer. As I left I couldn't help but think that one of the women I was dealing with was going to get me killed. No doubt about it, they were the same kind of crazy as me.

Chapter Twenty-Four

———

The next morning I talked to Brad Caylor, Merritt's boat dock chief, who I knew from when Alex had some issues on his first boat, Tyson's Pride. Brad told me that the Alex's lost Merritt had been found by Doug Whitman, who leased one of A.B.E. spaces at the Pompano Beach complex. He ran an undersea rescue operation and boat recovery service. In retrospect, I should have thought of Doug earlier. I decided to make that my first stop of the day.

The A.B.E. warehouse complex was an amalgamation of office and commercial businesses, with a series of "bays" in the rear portion. The fifty plus bays were a cornucopia of small enterprises, some renting multiple bays, from MaryAnn and Jackie's Car Detailing, to Bud's Harley Shop, to electricians and plumbers, to sundry enterprises which were just, or totally, beyond the law. Dean's actual job for A.B.E. was still managing and leasing the places, making him on a first name basis with all the tenants, including the Dade County Sheriff, who rented a store front for a satellite office.

One of the many businesses without a moniker, just a number, was Neptune Investigations, housed in Building B-17, Bays 3 and 4. I pulled in front seeing Doug Whitman leaning against the bay door reading a newspaper. Doug watched me as I stepped out of the car and yelled: "Quinn. By god it's good to see you."

Floridian all the way, dressed in khaki shorts, palm print shirt, deck shoes, holding a cup of Starbuck's coffee, and looking trim, sporting a short pulled back blond pony tail just out of the back of his Hurricane's ball cap. One of those south coasters who you're not sure if he is a multimillionaire or a bum. Whitman could have been either. He was an ex-Navy seal who, my guess, Alex set up in business. There was an endless stream of new boat owners negligently or intentionally sinking their boats. Their insurance carriers were financially interested in not only finding the boats, but knowing why they sunk.

We exchanged some small talk then walked into his bays which contained an assortment of gear, tanks, probes, sea-stuff, and fish-stuff, all very neatly stacked and spotless. Stopping at a stainless steel table with a life like moray eel, belly open, exposing not guts, but computer parts and small gears, I said: "What's with the mechanical fish?"

He said, cleaning his hands, pointing: "Elijah? We're doing an autopsy. The Navy seals found Elijah swimming around the carrier Ronald Reagan, off the Gulf of Yemen. One of the engineers at SeaWorld of Ohio built it about ten years ago for checking out their tanks. But take a look at that."

He handed me an enlarged photo of the inside of Elijah which showed Arabic marking of some kind.

He said: "The Navy wants us to take it apart and figure out how it was modified. Then trace all the parts that were changed, especially the non-metallic ones. They already have the two towel heads in Ohio who bought it a couple years ago under arrest."

He threw a cover over the mechanical fish, and said: "So to what do I owe the honor of your presence? Come down to shoot the breeze with old Dougie?"

"Not exactly. I heard you found Alex's boat."

"Yeah, Alex said you would be down."

I didn't press him on what Alex had told him to tell me. I said: "Where's it at?"

"It's still over at Cat. The Bahamians will milk this thing for at least another couple months before releasing it. I got photos if you want to look."

Pulling out a file, he laid out multiple color eight by ten prints on the table which I perused. Doug said: "Anything strike you odd about this wreck?"

I thought for moment, then said: "Well, there are no holes anywhere and it's pretty undamaged for being lost at sea, I guess."

126

"Good guess. I've only ever seen one other boat come up this clean. I was still with the Seals, instructing and training on undersea rescue of divers trapped in boats. We got our hands on yachts of different sizes confiscated for drug running. We decided to sink them and then set up situations where divers would be trapped inside, maybe on tanks, maybe just pockets of air, so we needed them intact. When you sink a boat like that so it will settle soft on the bottom on its beam, it takes a pro. We screwed up several, smashing the bow or stern, until we figured it out. You have to flood the aft cabins, and then slowly start with the rest of the boat, being careful you get it going down on the right angle so it doesn't corkscrew down. Actually, I figured it out playing with my sister's kid's bathtub toys. Submarine guys probably know how to do it as well. Alex's boat settled to the bottom like pro set it up."

"So why did you find it and no one else?"

"Whoever did this really knew the waters. You know the ledge out there and a little outcrop. Not a lot of people know about this because it's not fished very often because you can never get a good anchor. I just thought if I was going to sink a boat, that's where I would consider."

"Find anything inside that shouldn't have been there?"

"Like what?"

"Like bodies."

"The main door was left open, so anyone dead was shark dinner within an hour of going down. The 'cuda would get the rest."

"Anything else you can tell me?'

"Someone set off an explosion of some kind in the engine room, just behind the second diesel. I'd say while it was still a float, and my guess is it was loud, but there was no damage to speak of. Either someone wanted to scare someone, or they had explosives and didn't know how to handle them. Your guess either way is as good as mine."

He took a Dave Letterman sip of his coffee and said: "Really that's about it. Merrit's insurance boys are all giddy, thinking they're off the hook. CAT's diesel crew knew that it wasn't them anyway, and Alex, he just said to get it back to Merritt, clean it up and send the bill to his insurance company."

"So what's your hunch, who did it?"

He said: "Oh, I don't know. The drug boys over at Bimini are your first choice. Same bums who probably chased you. They steal these boats, sink'm with their drugs inside, then go back when they need them. Underwater storage. After that, it's stripped down piece by piece. Christ, the wood alone is worth a few hundred thousand, then the radar, the engines, and don't forget the gold crapper. But like I said before, this looks like a pro. I'm not sure the pot heads on Bimini could pull it off."

Doug showed me some more photos and explained how he thought it was sunk so as to be one piece. Also pointing out what was water damaged beyond repair. I was ready to leave and he said:

"One more thing I forgot."

He pulled out another set of photos and said to take a look. The photos were of a variety of personal property, fishing gear, poles, coolers, and what appeared to be junk. Not able to tell what I was to be looking for, I said: "What?"

Shuffling through the prints he handed me, pointing to the one in my hand and said: "See that?"

"A wet bag of clothes?"

"Sort of. A duffle bag, a luggage bag, and a backpack. The Bahamian's have all this stuff but we went through it. The luggage was the captain's. We couldn't tell about the backpack. No ID. But the duffle bag ID was a George Frampton. Alex said you might be interested in knowing that."

"How do you know it was his?"

"He had a money belt, with his name and address inside, maybe couple hundred dollars in it. Then a plastic water case with his Bahamian entry pass, a duplicate passport."

I thought but didn't say: "or someone wanted you to think it was his." I told Doug thanks and to let me know when they released the boat. I left, starting to get in the Mustang when my cell rang. It was Dean, who said: "Jake. I can see you from my window. How you doing?"

"Ok. Dean. What do you need?"

"Good. Good." Then a pause and I finally said,

exasperated:"What?"

"Hey. Thanks for taking my call. Can you stop over while you're here? I know you're busy. It will only take a few minutes. It's some corporate business. Come on, Jake, you can double bill it."

I didn't appreciate the double billing comment, but clients always get a kick out of messing with their lawyers. I told Dean I would be glad to and I hung up. My cell beeped with a voice mail. I checked the message which was a familiar voice:

"Jacob Bernard Quinn. So you're here in Florida and I haven't heard from you. Am I annoyed? Angry? What are these feelings? How about foolish. It's not good to make a girl feel foolish. But you've always been good at that. Haven't you?" End of message.

I had the feeling that just calling back and saying "I forgot to call" wasn't going to be near enough. But a few more hours weren't going to matter one way or the other. I decided to call her royal highness Trina Beckett back later, after I met with Dean.

As I walked through the parking lot, feeling the Florida sun starting to stoke its afternoon furnace. I thought about Doug's drug runner theory. It didn't wash with me. It just seemed too neat, too packaged. Maybe if I didn't have all the other stories swirling around, I wouldn't be suspicious. But why go to all this length to convince someone that your boat was stolen and sunk by drug runners?

Those thoughts, and a few more, as I swung open the doors to Office Building No. 1, which actually had a big "One" on the front. I had no idea where A.B.E. put all their money, but updating the Pompano Beach complex was not one of them. No need to as there was always a waiting list for the bays and cheap office space.

Dean's office was a single on the second floor as Trina had long since moved the corporate headquarters up to Boca Raton. Where could she get a decent lunch in Pompano without staring at seniors or tourists? Dean's secretary, Bonnie, had just gotten off the phone and told me that Dean was down the hall at the conference room waiting for me. I walked down seeing Trina and Alex's old offices, now filled with Bonnie's "kids": a mortgage broker, a cell phone salesman, the Recording Artist's Union, the one room law office of "Limpshaw and Foulton", and Tony Rumco, bail bondsman.

I walked into the conference room. Dean was at the far end with an open legal size box in the middle, five to six stacks of papers in front of him and a few more stacks on the floor. He got up as soon as I came in and said: "Hey, Jake, great, great. Coffee? No, No. You're a tea drinker, right. Did Bonnie get you some?"

"I'm good Dean." Skipping any social discourse: "What are you working on here?", said with a tone that I hope didn't reflect what I saw on Dean's face as he was looking at his stacks: a kid who had taken apart his Christmas toy and couldn't get it back together before Dad came home.

"Jake, this is what I think I need you to look at. Or at least get me going in the right direction."

He shuffled through one of the stacks and pulled out a letter and handed it to me. The letterhead revealed Sun Coast Bank, from the Commercial Lending Department and read:

Dunn and Bradstreet rating has down graded to B+ A.B.E.'s Mortgage in the amount of One Million Two Hundred Thousand Dollars ($1,200,000.00) on your commercial property located in Pompano Beach, Florida. As such, your loan rate will change effective immediately from Prime plus one, to Prime plus two.

He saw I was finished and said: "I knew this was coming. They called to tell me that all the problems up north that Trina was dealing with had reached the creditors. I don't care about the interest rate. You know me Jake, I don't get involved in the finances. I rent properties. Hell, let's face it, I'm the maintenance man and Alex's fishing mate. If they didn't pay me so much I'd have to find a real job. But lately I've never upgraded anything because I've been thinking of making an offer to buy the place. I had Bonnie pull all the corporate stuff and find out what my rights are since I am still an officer. Just when that's happening I get this letter from one of Trina's corporate lawyers in Boca."

He handed me another letter directed to Dean, this one from Attorney Carrie Habercorn:

As a Corporate officer of A.B.E, please accept this notice that the President, Trina Beckett, intends to call a Special Meeting of the Board of Directors within the next thirty days. Pursuant to the By-laws, Article 5, § 12, the President will attempt to accommodate a meeting time and date convenient to Directors. Prior to this meeting will be a meeting of the Beckett-McDonald Children's Voting Trust.

When Dean saw I was done reading he said: "Jake, I don't know what the hell is going on here. Habercorn is Trina's mouthpiece here in Florida. No point in me talking to Trina and I hope I can talk to Alex this week. I was wondering if you could look through the paperwork, or maybe you remember if I have any rights. They talked about giving me a right of first refusal, but I can't remember if anything ever came of that."

He scuffled papers again and said: "The stacks here are the Bylaws, the Buy/Sell, and the Children's Voting Trust, which I understand Alex holds for Trina and our kids. Look, I have to run down to show an office to a tenant. If you could look through this I'd really appreciate it."

I always seemed to be overly deferential to Dean, probably by way of guilt and said I would. I had drafted some of the documents, but not all. I reviewed the Bylaws, Buy/Sell, looked over the last several years minutes, not expecting to find anything there, and didn't. Dean had no right to buy the complex.

The Beckett Children's Voting Trust was next. Trina had referenced the Trust in the past when Alex and Trina were arguing over placing one of Alex's friends on the Board of Directors of a related company. The Trust was in control of Trina and her children's shares in A.B.E. and was set up as part of Alex's divorce settlement. There were no provisions concerning Dean, but one Section caught my attention, and wouldn't have except for the combination of letters Dean showed me. It read:

§ 15.5 Removal of Trustee: Rating

In the event that Dunn and Bradstreet rating for A.B.E. falls below A+ for a period of six months, the Trustee shall be removed and the alternate Trustee shall assume that position.

I quickly flicked through to the *Alternate Trustee* section not excepting a surprise, not getting one. It was simple. The Alternate Trustee: *Trina Beckett.*

I put the files back in order, walked down the hall seeing Dean chatting with Bonnie. He asked if I found anything and I told him nothing that I thought would help him. He should talk to Trina and Alex, maybe before getting a lawyer involved. I felt fairly sure that if either one got a call from a lawyer first, his day job would be driving a Miss Debbie truck. He thanked me and agreed. As I was walking out Bonnie said: "How'd you like Alex and Doug's new government project?"

I said, just pausing at the stairs to the first floor exit: "Alex and Doug's project?"

"So Doug gave you the impression that it was his? That's another one of Alex's deal. He had Congressman Taupin down here last month looking over the progress. I don't think Trina thinks it's a good idea. At least that's what she told Dean when she and the Congressman left for lunch. Or wherever together."

She ended that with a grin that girls master as a teenager when having the pleasure of informing an unsuspecting lad that his girlfriend is two timing him. I nodded a response, which was: I got the message.

At that moment, getting in the Mustang, that old weakness didn't seem so strong.

Chapter Twenty-Five

Not getting an answer on my cell call to Island Air, I drove over to find out if they were flying the next day. Christine Dodd of the Weather Channel had described a morning depression fermenting just off the Keys, heading north east toward Cat Cay. I was brewing my own depression grousing about Trina, as I passed red Mercedes, silver Lexus's and the new status symbol: yellow Hummers. Capitalist democracy depends on third generation extravagance: unearned wealth pissed away until economic equilibrium is returned. Sometimes the little bastards can't spend it all in a lifetime, which is why the government helps by imposing death taxes.

On my way to Island Air I stopped at Tony's Pawn Shop at the edge of Browntown. I kept a locker at Tony's and when I came in Tony and I chatted about the weather, as I handed him my key. Private lockers with guns near airports was a by product of airport security checks and I had set this one up two years ago in another case for Alex. He went to the back to my "box" and returned with my Glock 30 handgun and Anson ankle holder. Strapping the ankle holder around my right ankle, I checked the Glock to make sure the clip was full and the safety was on. The Glock, bought on Moot's recommendation, was as small as a 22, but significantly more powerful. And it had a great safety, so I wouldn't shoot my toes off.

When I got to Island Air I was told all flights were on hold due to the weather and to check back later. The frustration of lost time lead me back to Parker's for lunch, intentionally skirting the lunch crowd. Mo was wearing more of a country outfit: jeans, short top and vest. On her left shoulder was an indiscernible tattoo that Bryan would surely covet. Across me at the bar sat two dry wall contractors arguing about whether the movie *Jackie Brown* was based on the book *Rum Punch* by Elmore Leonard. I knew the answer, but didn't offer.

I ordered a Rolling Rock and chowder, pulled a pen from my pocket, turned over the paper ad placemat Mo had put down, and started a laundry list of random thoughts. I sketched out names and events: Trina, Alex, Taupin, Tad, Frampton's, Zero, Whitman, Palm pilot, Corning, nano-tech, Homeland, CIA, iJet, Defense, Diane. I circled some, underlined others and then started drawing lines to connect names and maybe events. Frampton didn't seem too complicated to me: show her the money. Alex was too smart to be leveraged by Frampton, or Frampton's, for that matter. I noticed I was making concentric circles around Trina's name. Why the special meeting to get control of a voting trust? But none of this helped me figure out who killed Tad or where the palm pilot really fit in.

Half way through another "33", a guy sporting Harley insignias came in through the back and sat down a couple stools to my right. He looked like a One Percenter, that tag given, or taken, by the group of riders who don't pretend the bad boy image, they lived it. Standard attire blue jeans, white tee, black leather vest with assorted pins, blond hair with pony tail, and short cut goatee. Maybe mid-twenties and seemingly vaguely familiar. But most biker's do look familiar, all wearing the same tribal outfits.

Mo flashed a familiar smile and poured a small glass of water and a shot of Maker's Mark. He took a sip of both and went behind the bar to a shelf where Lou kept his daily newspapers: The Miami Herald, the NY Daily News and the Wall Street Journal. I was guessing Daily News, which goes to show you, because he came back with the Journal. Taking another sip of the Maker's Mark, he said to me: "You follow stocks much?"

I said: "A little, but a lot less over the last couple years."

He rubbed his chin, a goat tee-er's habit and said: "Harley stock article. Says that the Hundred Anniversary models sold well, but now they don't have a waiting list. First time."

He said to Mo: "Time to sell your Harley before it's too late."

Mo said: "You buying Dan?"

"If you go with it."

"I don't think you can afford me *and* the bike." Mo said smiling.

He smiled back, folded the article portion of the paper, and laid it to his left, my right, and started to look at another section not waiting or apparently wanting my reaction. Had Harley stock finally had its run? Curious as anyone who's owned a Harley and sold it, thinking a good thing can't last forever, I said: "Mind if I read the article?"

"Be my guest."

The article was in the center column and, as "Dan" said, Harley was having trouble with this year's model. Glancing through the first page I turned to A5-Col. 4 to continue. When I turned the page, where the article started, there was a small Post-it Note. The note read:

Diane asked me to contact you. Finish the article. Go out the back door. Ride the Harley out to Okees. Diane says she's run out of cigarettes.

A Bahaman stamp, similar to the one Bryan bought and with the Tad letter, was stuck on the note as well. No covert operative, yet I still knew enough not to look over his way. Diane sent this guy? What proof did I have of that? How did he know me well enough that I would read this article? Either he was legit or it was a set up with someone knowing about my contact with Diane, which could be anyone. I sat staring at the Journal, collecting my thoughts, and after a few minutes laid the paper back beside him and said: "Thanks. Maybe it's a good time to sell my bike?"

"Could be." He said.

I put a twenty down on the bar and causally walked back to the rear of the restaurant, past the dishwashers, to a door, where two Mexicans were sitting in the alley on garbage cans smoking cigarettes. At the corner of the back of the building was a Blue-Grey Harley Road King. The engine was still warm and the ignition not locked. I put my leg over the seat, hands on the bars, tilted the bike up to level, switched the ignition on, toed up to neutral, pushed the kill switch to start, opened the choke to half, pulled slightly down on the throttle, and hit the start button. It turned over with that sweet alternating patented throaty Harley sound. I kicked the gear shift lever forward into first and rolled out the alley onto the highway heading to Okees.

Okees was an old bar at the end of the Hillsboro Canal which ran from Lake Okeechobee to just above the inlet at Boca Raton. Spiced clams, stale beer and lousy service were its specialty. I made my way to Interstate 91 north toward Coral Springs, up 441 to Hillsboro Canal Boulevard, a straight stretch of isolated highway running along the Canal. That straight stretch was easy riding and I lost myself in the gears and sounds for a few minutes to Okees. I pulled in, parked the bike, and headed over to the deck that surrounded the restaurant. I tried looking around without being too obvious. I didn't spot my Wall Street Journal companion. I went to the outside window, ordered a beer and walked over to watch some of the odds and ends small crafts that meander out of Lake Okeechobee down the canal.

About ten minutes later the Mustang rental pulled up and parked beside the Harley. "Dan", walked over to me. I reached into my right pants pocket checking my keys. Seeing me do this, he threw me the keys, and said: "Took'm out of your pocket at the Bar." He walked past me and said: "Take a walk with me."

He had the straight forward voice of a young man who was comfortable with command. A different edge than the Harley act at the Parker. We walked up a concrete walkway which ran parallel to the canal to the end of dock area, a graveyard for discarded boats and pontoons. There was an old day runner sail boat in the mix. He smiled and said: "I learned to sail on one just like that up east. Just too much of a motor head. Why wait for a breeze? You sail?"

"No. Too much work for the few seconds of calm."

"Got that right."

I looked at the other boats, waiting for him to say more, hoping to wait him out for an explanation of why I was his guest near the entrance to the Okee swamps. I finally said: "So why the note?"

"What do you think?"

"Maybe you wanted to see if I was dumb enough to walk into a trap?"

"Are you?"

"Apparently if you're not working for Diane." I said.

"You don't work for Diane, just with her. She asked me to put my ear to the ground in our nation's capital."

Now it made some sense as I remembered Diane's last comment that she had someone in Washington poking around. I said: "Congressman Taupin doesn't think there are any problems. Says the government could care less about Frampton or the palm pilot. Should be all wrapped up nice and neat as soon as I meet with the insurance company."

He looked at me more directly and said: "Could be. But I don't think you believe that anymore than I did when I saw that bullshit note."

I didn't respond. He could sense that his knowledge of the note peeked my interest and his credibility. He said: "Let me give you a crash course. Have a seat."

We sat down on a flipped over pontoon and he said: "After 9/11 the FBI, CIA and DEA, god knows how many other agencies, set up the civilian equivalent of Delta strike teams. Small units highly trained and mostly filled with ex-Seals and Rangers. In theory, they're supposed to be under Homeland Security's tent, but no one believes that. These guys mean business and were set up like the terrorists: individual cells, from one man to no more than six, designed for long or short term missions. They're given an assignment, a target and set free. No Congressional investigation, no CNN Special Report, no interview with Wolf Blitzer."

He stopped and put a small chew under his lip. Moved it around in his mouth a bit, wiped his hands on his jeans and said: "Diane hates that. I tell her its part of the bit."

"And these teams are after the palm pilot and Frampton?" I said.

"In the beginning, Corning made so much noise about their stupid missing pilot that the FBI got interested. Then the CIA found out the FBI was interested so they wanted in because Frampton's a foreigner. Some underling at Homeland caught wind so they put two teams out for their own investigation. Ridge was kept out of the loop, until he got a call from Bert Tad. He was pissed off and ordered them all down."

"What about the operation in Bimini?"

"The CIA was using Tad's old scuba company at Bimini and they were the guys off Alex Beckett's shoreline every day. It was just a training operation, but when intel came across that the Corning palm pilot was in their waters one the teams took it on themselves to find it."

"If they're called back, then who's following me and what's going on?" I said.

"One of the reasons I took that gem of a rental was to see who was following you."

"And."

"You're being followed. But it's probably amateurs. Could be the FBI. Their arrogance makes them think they're invisible. Might be a private contractor. Either way I wouldn't worry about them. Let's walk back."

We got up and started walking back to the car and bike. He said: "You do need to worry about one thing."

"What's that?"

He said, nearing the bike, throwing his leg over: "First, be sure you know how to use that Glock on your ankle."

I smiled and said: "What else?"

"Homeland believes not everyone's been called back. There's a rogue out there still looking for the pilot and Frampton. Real interested. So much so Homeland's looking for him as well."

Letting that sink in, he started the bike. He said, loudly over the pipes: "You know this used to be a great place to a catch fish. You just needed the right bait. But it has to be alive when you put in the water. Be careful."

Rolling the throttle, he released the clutch and within a few seconds his image evaporated into the heat from the pavement.

I pulled out my keys and got into the rental. On the steering wheel was another hand written note: "Jake, be careful. Diane." The old sign at Okee's covered my rearview mirror as I pulled out: *Live Bait.*

Chapter Twenty-Six

———

Driving back to the Marriott, I called my office to check on messages. Eva gave me the current list of clients she was telling half truths to about the status of their file, then said: "Moot called all worked up about an article in the Tribune. I attached it to your e-mail. Said to read it."

"What's it about?"

"I said, you better read it." Finished with the scold, she said: "Brian called. You're to check your email for some information he had for you on Frampton and Alex. Said it was important."

"Ok. Anything else?"

"You get into trouble with the law down there in the Sunshine State?"

"Not yet. Why?"

"The Dade County Sheriff Duke McManus called and asked for you to call ASAP. Said he didn't want to have to pick you up. He seemed like a nice guy. Has a daughter at Florida State. His wife sells Amish furniture on the weekends."

I interrupted: "Eva, that's nice. If I relocate down here I'll remember to vote for him. You wouldn't have maybe asked him what he wants to pick me up for, would you?"

She said tersely: "Oh, right. I'll skip the rest. All the stuff that might help you understand him better. Maybe smooth some conversation with the man who can lock your ass up."

I didn't say anything, waiting her out and she finally gave me the number, refusing any more information about the Sheriff. Parting "best of friends", I dutifully told her I would call later in the week. She said she would try to find time to fit me in.

As I walked into the Marriott lobby the Pakistani desk clerk called me over, handing me a letter delivered while I was out. The crisp water mark envelope's return address was Peters and

Marks, Suite 12, Palmetto Drive, Boca Raton, Florida. Inside were a letter and a Release. I read the letter first:

Attorney Quinn:
Attached is a Full Release for your client, Elizabeth Frampton, along with a photocopy of the insurance proceeds check in full. The check is at our offices in Boca Raton. Have her sign the Release and then deliver it to the office to collect the check. I'll be there until 4:30 pm today. Thomas Graham. Esq.

I reviewed the Release which was standard fair with no representations as to status of deceased, George Frampton, dead or alive. I asked the desk clerk for directions up to Palmetto Drive, dutifully given.

Boutique satellite offices for large northeast law firms were set up to serve a few well healed clients who move themselves, but not their companies, South. The offices were typically manned by one or two attorneys and consisted usually of one secretary, a conference room and attorney office. Peters and Marks second floor suite was just that: large swinging glass doors with the name small but conspicuous. Entering into a small reception area was the tanned secretary behind a large opulent counter, giving the illusion that there were multiple conference rooms and offices behind the gatekeeper. I approached and asked if Attorney Graham was in. She quizzed me as to who I was and then politely lied that she would have to check. She proceeded to walk me ten steps past the conference room into an office where Graham was setting behind a desk, standing as I entered.

"Quinn. You got my note. Have a seat." I hesitated and he sensed it sounded like a command, so he said, surprisingly: "Please."

His tone was acerbic, but not harsh, which threw me off. I took a seat and said: "I don't have a signature yet, because I just got the Release, but I'm certain she will sign."

He reached into his briefcase, pulled out a check and handed it to me, saying: "Here's the check. My instructions were to deiiver it either way. We would like to have the Release but it doesn't really matter."

I looked at him for a moment, neither one of us saying anything until I said: "So why'd you come down here to see me?'

He struggled with the question, saying: "I've never really liked you Quinn. I don't really know why. Probably because you represent a threat. You're who I really want to be, you're a fucking mirror. But as much as I don't like you or your style of law, or for that matter your whining clients, I have no ill will for you personally."

"That's nice to know. Your therapist tells you to have this heart to heart with me?"

"I came down here to warn you. It's that simple. The problem is I don't know exactly from what."

He glanced at his watch. Putting some other files in his briefcase, he said: "I told you before, I don't see the merits of your client's claim. Certainly not at this point. There are so many outstanding investigations and questions into Frampton's disappearance there is no reasonable basis whatsoever to pay."

"So why the check?"

"I protested. Wrote an objection memo that once we pay, if Frampton shows up, which I know he will and so do you, she keeps the money. My memo gets circulated and Marks stands behind me at first. Then a few days ago he calls me into his office and tells me to settle. I resist. He tells me to settle or the file will be removed from my desk. I'm thinking of making a stand on this, thinking maybe Marks wants me to, as he is trapped by the client, but I can force the issue. Be the inside hired gun. I email to a senior adjuster at CNI suggesting that all these bad legal things might happen if they settle, which are of course true."

He began nervously rubbing his hands, talking louder: "A day after the email, I get visitors, not at my office, but at my home. My home for Christ's sake! Ten at night, kids in bed, and Annie and I watching the news. No identification, black car, black suits, white shirts, sunglasses, real Hollywood. Three men and one woman. Said they needed to talk to me, and that Annie should hear it as well. When one sat down he made sure I saw his gun and holster under his coat. They informed me that more was at stake in the Frampton case than I was aware of. That certain "wheels" were being put in motion and that if I was concerned about my career, and my life style, that I needed to rethink my position and quit sending emails. Listen to my boss and get the case settled. Did I understand? And of course the conversation never took place, don't call anyone, etc."

He lowered his voice, glancing to make sure the secretary was not around the corner. "I told them to get out. As they were walking out the door they said for me to think it over. If I had any doubts I should think about Susan Faldo."

I remembered Susan Faldo's name. Seven or eight years ago she was front page news in Pittsburgh and a topic around the County Bar Associations about excess billing. I said: "I met her once, seemed like a decent lawyer. Wasn't she disbarred though?"

"Actually suspended, which was later rescinded, but no difference. Her career was over. She was with our firm and we represented Thomas Piper, the timber operator from your neck of the woods who claimed the Department of Interior at the Allegheny National Forest was conspiring with International Paper to run him out of business. He challenged the constitutionality of certain OSHA logging safety regulations and was going to get a favorable ruling at least at the District Level."

I said, thinking more about it and remembering some newspaper articles: "She was also indicted, wasn't she, for mail fraud?"

"A la Webster Hubbell from Clinton's Rose law firm. The indictment listed work *our* firm did on a federal government contract case years before when she was an associate. We had to pull her off Piper's file and I took it over. She told me that shortly before she had been indicted she had been visited by the Assistant United States Attorney and two gentlemen who appeared to be FBI agents. She was told to accept their ridiculous offer on the case, with a stipulation not to challenge the new OSHA forestry regulations. If she did not, her client would "suffer the consequences" and the "gloves would come off." She threw them out and started filing Freedom of

Information Act Petitions in Washington to find out more about the new regulations and her visitors. A week later she was led out of her office at the Oxford Center in handcuffs. Front page of the Pittsburgh Post Gazette."

"Didn't Tommy John represent her?" I said. Tommy John was a white collar crime attorney out of Pittsburgh who Alex had on retainer and who I knew through Trina.

"Yeah. We hired Tommy for her, but the feds had a mountain of her time slips, computer entries and accounts receivables all documenting double billing, right off her laptop. While that was going on, Pipers suddenly was audited by the IRS, Pennsylvania DEP started doubling his bonds, shutting down jobs and the Department of Labor tripled his workers compensation rates. We had no choice but to settle. Within weeks, the audits disappeared, DEP lowered his bonds, his rates went down, and he was awarded an exclusive ten year Allegheny National Forest timber contract. Right after Piper settles, Susan's indictment is withdrawn as the United States Attorney discovered a computer error and all new documents appear that support Susan's billing. No apology, but it didn't matter, she had been suspended from our firm, never to return and had a shambles of career left behind."

"Whatever happened to her?"

He said, noticeably dismal: "I'm still in touch. Susan has a small general practice near the Monroeville Mall. A waste of talent. I help her out with some referrals, but she's lost her nerve."

He closed his briefcase and said: "Here's the thing. These guys obviously knew all about Susan's case. They were letting me know that whoever they were, they were behind Susan's downfall, and if I continued to fuck around with this petty insurance claim the same fate would befall me."

He stopped and buzzed the secretary to make sure the cab was out front. He said turning back to me: "Anyway, after my nighttime visit, I saw Marks in the morning, which was yesterday. All he said was: You were told to settle, either do it today or leave the firm immediately. No other discussion. I booked the nine thirty this morning out of Pittsburgh to West

Palm and here I am."

"So why tell me this story?"

"I'm not sure. Guilt? Pride? Embarrassment? I don't know. I don't feel good about folding and walking away. But I have a family. Maybe I'm a coward, something I don't think you are. I thought you should know why your client's getting this check and know who you are dealing with. I haven't had a lot of friends in my career. Susan was one of them. I should have protected her."

He picked up his briefcase and said: "I have to go Quinn. Good luck. Drop off the Release when you get it. One more thing."

"What's that?"

"There is another policy on Frampton for one million and your client's the beneficiary. I take it she didn't tell you about that. They're paying that as well."

No handshake. He walked past me, leaving me in the office as I heard him say to his secretary that he was leaving and would see her again sometime. I walked out sticking the check for one hundred thousand in my shirt pocket. Another million? There were plenty of women who would think about exchanging their husband for that extra zero. Elizabeth Frampton was one of them.

Lawyer to lawyer they might mislead you, but they're not supposed to lie to you. Hell, that's the way it ought to be. Right?

Chapter Twenty-Seven

—

I decided to drive to A.B.E. at Pompano Beach and use their computer to retrieve my email from Moot and Bryan. Trina's office was closer in Boca, but I was still not ready for that impending confrontation. On the drive I thought that trusting anyone and any story was becoming a problem. I had never trusted Graham before but had to accept his warning for what it was. Parking, I noticed some Sheriff's deputies in front of their office. They looked my way and I ignored them.

Bonnie was at her desk and she said I could use her computer to check my email as she had some errands to run. I could answer the phone too, if I didn't mind. Getting on line, I retrieved my email, pulling up messages from Moot and Brian along with attachments. I opened Moot's first:

Jake: Attached is an article in the Greensburg Trib about Zero. I called him but haven't heard back. Who or what are we dealing with here? ---Moot.

The attachment was part of the article from the front page of the Tribune:

District Attorney Subject of FBI Probe

The Tribune has learned today that Otis "Zero" Nageli is the subject of an FBI probe. The FBI issued a statement that they do not comment on "on-going" investigations, that it "did not necessarily mean that the District Attorney was a target of the investigation", but that arrest warrants "were a possibility depending on the level of cooperation." Yesterday, Federal

Marshall's served warrants on the District Attorney's office, seizing his personal computer. Sources have stated that the inquiry is related to Homeland Security investigation and may involve child pornography.

The District Attorney stated: *"Our office has been conducting an investigation into a local death that obviously has the federal government nervous. Apparently they have little regard for the first amendment over there in Pittsburgh. Let me tell the Feds, Zero hasn't even begun to take his shots yet."*

The feds had picked the wrong guy to intimidate, but I suspected that was just their opening maneuver. I closed that file and clicked on the email from Bryan:

Jake: I won't tell you how I got this but let's just say that wireless and firewall are incompatible. Enjoy. Hope it helps. Brian

It was an internal Schwab Brokerage Memo reading:

Confidential

IPO Alert: Schwab Analysts have completely downgraded to "Avoid", the Initial Public Offering of Ovonics (OVA, Offer price: $20.00). Insiders are growing sour after confirmation of payment of death benefits to the widow of George Frampton, confirming his rumored death. Frampton was the driving principal in the innovative nano technology of this speculative venture. Morgan/Stanley is the broker and underwriter and it is virtually assured now that this offer will never get through the pipeline to be offered to the public.

Morgan/Stanley may still be obligated to one of the principal investors, Alex Beckett, a fifty percent owner. Morgan/Stanley was committed to purchase five million shares of Beckett's at ten dollars a share, which will result in a liability to Morgan/Stanley of fifty million dollars.

146

While still on line I dialed Bryan on his cell. He answered and I said: "Can you tell me what this Schwab memo means?"

"Sure. The public offering folded and Alex is going to get rich, or should I say richer, for it. He worked a deal with the underwriter Morgan/Stanley that even if the company does not go public Morgan/Stanley must buy five million of Alex's shares at ten bucks a share."

"Why would Morgan Stanley get in a deal like that?"

"Happens all the time. Morgan/Stanley figured they would make money when they sold it to the public for twenty a share. But obviously with Frampton dead, the whole thing unraveled and Alex is going to cash in."

I quickly told Bryan I had to go and went off line, deleting the material, as the two deputies I saw earlier walked out of the elevator. Police always come in twos: one short, one tall, or one skinny, one fat, or one with hair, one bald or one mean, one nice. These two had it all: a tall, young, good looking, thin, chap, and a balding, fat, ugly little twerp. Of course the stereotype didn't fit as the tall one said bluntly: "Sheriff McManus wants to see you right now."

I gave him a stare and grin that the smaller could sense meant, "Show me a warrant asshole", so he interceded and said: "Don't mind Elvis here, he just came off a midnight. The Sheriff *asked* to see you. You're in his town, you know the drill."

I said: "Fine. Show me the way."

We walked across two parking lots to the Sheriff's branch office in Building No. 3 at the end of the complex. Nothing elaborate. Steel desks, half partitions, lockers, and commercial green carpet. I was led into a small partitioned area in the back. The Sheriff was getting off the phone. Sheriff Duke McManus was probably forty to forty-five, showing some white around the ears, trim, dressed in khakis, golf shirt with Sheriff logo, and no gun. Motioning me to sit down, he hung up and reached across the desk with a hand, saying: "Mr. Quinn, thanks for coming to see me. I appreciate it."

There was nothing voluntary about me being there. In police terms anything less than handcuffs are voluntary.

I said: "Elvis needs some lessons in public relations."

"He's a good kid. Had a brother killed two months ago in a raid on a drug ring down the road from your complex here. He'll come around, if he can push through. He's just covering the fear and dealing with the loss with anger. Hopefully he can make it or I'll have to have him serving subpoenas or watching juries."

In the Southern States, the Sheriff carried a big stick, unlike up north where the Sheriff mainly served process and provided security for the court. Here the Sheriff had a multimillion dollar budget and a staff in the hundreds. Often a stepping stone to higher office as well.

I said: "Well, I certainly feel like an insensitive shit now. What do you need from me Sheriff?"

"I don't know." Said in a quizzical manner, seeming to ask himself the question. At the same time, he reached in a leather briefcase leaning against the side of his desk and pulled out a folder. Everywhere I went people were pulling out folders. He opened it, flipped through some papers and said: "I'm not sure how to start this with you. Alex says you're a straight shooter. I'll assume he's right unless you show me otherwise."

He flipped through some more papers, stopped and said: "We found Elizabeth Frampton dead last night at her apartment."

I sensed the sheriff was looking for a reaction. I didn't have one. Just a vision of her face the last time I saw her.

"Did you know that?" He said.

"No."

"I didn't think so. I hope my guess about that is right for your sake."

The phone rang. Perturbed at being interrupted he answered, shook his head, said "Yeah", a few times, put the phone down, and got up. As he went around his desk, he said: "Here's the preliminary report, read it and I'll be right back." He pushed the file over to my side of the desk.

The report was less professional than most up north, reflecting, my guess, and fewer veteran detectives. I scanned the ten pages and pieced together the police version of what happened.

Elizabeth Frampton had called the apartment manager last night to ask whether anyone had been let into her apartment without her knowledge. The manager said not that he was aware of. She told him she had an early flight out of town the next morning and to tell the cleaning woman to clean out the refrigerator for her. She said she would leave extra money on the counter. The next morning, the cleaning woman found Elizabeth Frampton dead, under water in her bathtub, unclothed, a small cut on side of the head, half filled wine glass on the side of the tub. The manager called the sheriff, forensics did what they do and a detective took statements and wrote the report. He noted the extra cleaning money was still on the counter. Initial conclusion: accidental death, slipped in tub. Wait for toxicology and autopsy.

As I finished, the Sheriff walked in, sat down and said: "Nice and neat isn't it? Normally we would just chalk this up as another accident. People don't get too excited about these things unless there's a gun involved. But Alex Beckett draws big water in this town. And this was his latest girl and the gossip mill will be grinding out some stories soon and then maybe some snotty reporter wanting to make a name for herself starts asking around about how we handled this. We need to cover all the bases."

"Have you talked to Alex?" I said.

"Not yet. Can't get a hold of him."

"So why are you talking to me?"

"Couple of reasons. First, our detectives have been snooping around and you and deceased were seen at Lou Parker's early in the evening. That right?"

"I didn't know meeting with your client made you a murder suspect?"

He smiled, leaning back in his chair. "Might make you a witness though. We know she hired you to collect some insurance money for her missing husband. Did she tell you if anyone threatened her or if she owed anyone any money?"

I was under no obligation to tell the sheriff anything and he knew it. I said: "Look Sheriff, I don't know anything about her death. Frankly, I don't think I can help you. You knew I wasn't going to say anything when I walked in. Why haul me in here? Why let me read the report?"

"Like I said earlier, I know Alex Beckett. He's done me some favors. I owe him. But there's a line. The way I see it, this is a homicide. I got three suspects right now: her husband, Alex Beckett or Beckett's daughter Trina."

The mention of Trina made my eyes twitch ever so slightly and the Sheriff noticed it, saying: "You saw the sanitized report, you know that. The rest is still in the detective's head. He'll put it down in writing when he needs to. We already ran a check with the FBI. They're real interested in people with passports. Even Brits. They're not convinced her husband's dead. You're not part of an insurance scam, are you Mr. Quinn?'

Normally I would have walked out, but I was in too deep. I said: "I'll let that pass for now. But you're starting to piss me off."

He continued smiling: "You might want to know that we checked the dearly departed's cell phone records right before she was killed. She made a bunch of calls. Travel agents, airlines, banks. One to Lou Parker's even, that's how we found out about your meeting. Two others: Trina Beckett, earlier in the evening for five minutes. And one to Alex, just a message. I'll tell you what   she   said."

"Wait a minute." I said interrupting. "Don't you guys believe in warrants?"

"Don't need one under the Patriot Act. You want to know or not?"

I nodded affirmatively.

"She said, quote: "He's looking for the pilot. Ask your lawyer. Be careful. Sorry Alex. Have a nice life." He waited a few seconds and said: "Now I don't know who the pilot is, but I'll find out soon enough. You can save me a lot of investigative work and tell me why Alex is supposed to talk to you about the pilot?"

The FBI had not told him about the "palm pilot" and I saw no need to enlighten him. I didn't answer.

He said: "Suit yourself. Let me give you some advice. My loyalty to Alex goes only so far. I'll do what I can for him, but covering up a murder is not on the list. I haven't been able to get a hold of Alex or Trina yet. I suggest you talk to them and tell them to cooperate."

I got up from my chair and said: "I'll do that. We done, Sheriff?"

"For now. As they say in the movies: don't leave town."

As I turned to walk out, he said: "One more thing. We bagged the dead woman's hands. Forensics came up with some skin under one of her finger nails. Just thought you should know."

"Thanks." I said.

As I left the front door, walking to my car, I fought reaching to my neck and wondered if my shirt collar hid the scratch marks of Elizabeth Frampton. I needed some room to breathe.

Chapter Twenty-Eight

——

Walking across the parking lot past the entrance to Dean's offices, I stopped and leaned against a window at a non-descript storefront. A young secretary was outside the office smoking a cigarette and I could have used one. Nice list of suspects. Elizabeth Frampton's husband, the killer? Good possibility if he was alive. There certainly was enough money floating around to bring back the dead. But the Sheriff wasn't leaving out Trina or Alex. Or me for that matter. A forensic expert with a degree from the back of old matchbook cover could tie me to the murder scene with Elizabeth's parting gesture to me. How long would it be before I was served with a warrant for a DNA sample?

Trina in a gold digger confrontation with Frampton was a possibility, but murder seemed a stretch. Alex was a better suspect and the Sheriff knew that as well. Was Elizabeth holding that much information on Alex to provide motive for murder? Alex would have been neater about it. Whoever killed her might have killed Tad and that had to eliminate Alex. Unless the goal was to pin this on Alex.

I needed some time I didn't have to sort all this out when a red two door BMW 525 roared up in front of me. The woman in the driver's seat pointed to the passenger door, so I walked over, opened the door and got in. She backed up and as we headed out the lot, south on Pompano Boulevard, I said: "Trina. How are you?"

She stared ahead not revealing if she was angry or contemplating a cleaver response.

I said: "Where we going?"

After a left at the next corner on to I-90 North, I got the following: "You would think for the amount of money we pay you, you'd at least tell me where you've been."

Her tone belied a professional indiscretion. Making it personal. Her shifting from business to personal was wearing thin, but that's what you get when you mix the two. I needed to get off the personal side if I was going to get anywhere, and anywhere was information about just what Trina was up to. I said:

"Elizabeth Frampton was murdered last night."

Her foot went off the gas and she stared over at me, expressionless, that half look suggesting: you're kidding right. She said: "Where at? How?"

"At her apartment. They don't know who did it. Do you?'

Silent she turned into the Riviera Coast Country and Yacht Club giving a straight-up smile to the guard, followed by an unpleasant glance at me. She made her way past the golf course to the three acre coast lot with the Frank Lloyd Wright designed home she and Dean bought fifteen years earlier. Wright designed the home in the forties and in the seventies the land surrounding was sold off to build Riviera Coast. A four foot stone fence surrounded the acreage. She pulled her BMW through the arched entrance, up the circular driveway to the front. She didn't say anything further, got out and I followed.

No comfort zone in this house for me, although I had been inside many times. It was Trina and Dean's home at one time. She kept the house, not finding one with more style and a better view. With the kids gone the house was closing in and the social scene no longer to her liking. As with all Wright homes, Frank never compromised his "visual" themed architecture, leaving little room for later modification. Narrow, tight gallery hallways and a small stone enclosed circular kitchen in the middle made for lousy entertaining. But who was there to entertain anymore?

Trina made her way to the small stone bar fixing herself a drink saying: "Need a drink?"

"Sure." I said.

She poured me a Captain Morgan Private Stock and herself a Grey Goose gimlet, both on the rocks. I stepped out onto the flagstone patio, blending into the manicured lawn, then her empty dock and the Atlantic. Handing me the drink, I noticed she was dressed in tight black pants, red low cut silk top, with a small diamond necklace that I think, not sure, I bought for her several years ago. Just a touch of make-up. Had me wishing I had started our evening on the lighter side. Telling someone they're a suspect in a murder was not a good mood setter, unless maybe you're the murderer.

She took a long sip, staring at the ocean, then turned to me and said: "So you want to know what I know about poor Elizabeth Frampton's untimely demise. Well, actually, nothing. So you think I was involved?"

"It doesn't matter what I think, but the Sheriff's got you and your father on a short list of suspects."

"Me?" with a voice, not of indignation, but surprise.

I carved the next question to push her, letting her think the Sheriff had these thoughts: "Daddy's princess killing his mistress gold digger would play well to a jury. Or how about a CEO who wanted to eliminate someone who knew too much? Or a simple cat fight?"

Rimming her glass with a finger, staring at me, pacing a response, she finally said: "I was there last night. She had called, said she had information on my father that I needed to know about the company. So I went over."

"How long were you there?"

"I'd say half an hour. I didn't kill her if that's what you think."

"What'd she want to tell you?"

"Nothing really. When I walked in it was obvious she was leaving for somewhere as she had her bags out. The whole thing was uncomfortable because I can't stand the rotten bitch. Don't even know why, she's really no different than the rest. Thought I was numb to them all. She offered me some wine. I asked where she was traveling to. She said back to England, quote: 'For a while, maybe longer. Maybe forever.' Somewhere along the way, she started talking about Enron and Martha Stewart going to prison and how difficult that would be for someone rich. I thought the whole conversation was disjointed. But then she got around to it."

"Which was?"

"A threat. Said she had plenty of information on my father and our companies that the stock authorities would like to have. Enough to put my father in jail for a very long time and destroy the company. She said if she was left alone, none of it would come out. At least not from her. But if Alex came after her, she would tell everything she knew."

She turned away, looking out the window waiting for me. I said: "And?"

"I called her bluff, told her to go ahead, that was his problem, not mine. She didn't flinch. She laughed at me. Asked if I wanted to take the chance. Then the conversation got ugly."

"Physical?"

"I said the conversation got ugly. I left. That was it."

"Did you touch anything else besides the glass?"

"I don't know? Not really."

"Anyone know you were going there or see you there?"

"The manager, I guess. I couldn't find the apartment so he pointed it out to me. How'd she die?"

"They're not sure. Probably hit over the head and made it look like she fell in the bathtub. Not a professional job."

"Not very creative either."

"Most homicides aren't." Said with a confidence I didn't have.

"Maybe you ought to quit the Jack Web routine and tell me what else the sheriff told you. You are on my dime."

I told her of the sheriff wanting me to be a warning messenger to her father. She thought Alex was capable of killing Elizabeth Frampton but anyone was if pushed hard enough. We talked briefly about the mystery of Frampton's missing husband but had no conclusions, like everyone else. It was as good a time as any to confront Trina about some other issues. I said: "I met with Dean today."

"Yeah I know, he told me."

"So what's up with getting control of the Trust? She threaten you about that as well?"

"I wondered when you would get around to something that's none of your business."

"Wait a minute. You bring me in concerning all these

government intrusions into your company, you become a suspect in a homicide, now you tell me it's none of my business. You damn well owe me some explanation."

"You're the lawyer. We don't owe you an explanation of anything."

She was emphatic and angry. She had been waiting for my inquiry. Always one step ahead, just like her father. I said: "The apple doesn't fall far from the tree, does it?"

"You think I am so evil. Like my father. You don't know me, even, after all this time."

She turned again to windows with her back to me, maybe hiding tears, but I doubted it. Hug or humor? Maybe something clever with a hug. I chose silence. Finally she said: "Let's take a walk, know it all."

"Where to?"

"Just grab us a couple drinks."

I got us both another drink and I followed her around the side of the house to where some of the palms turned into a thicket. We walked down a small lane, golf cart wide, with flowers and a few bench cut outs along the way, past a little pond. After a few minutes, still on her property, there was an opening with a small cottage, patio, again looking to the ocean. Similar style as to her Wright house but more modern. She walked ahead of me, went to the door, didn't knock, opened it, and walked in saying: "Doris? It's Trina."

Following, I saw a woman dressed casually in slacks, probably in her sixties coming through the patio door saying: "Hi, Mrs. Beckett. We're in the backyard."

"Doris, are you ever going to start calling me Trina?"

She just smiled back, the answer obviously no. Trina motioned for me to follow her to the patio where there were several tables and umbrellas, facing the ocean. Sitting at the table was a stately woman, my guess sixty, her fair skin and perfect short light hair making it hard to tell. She sat with a series of small wooden carved blocks in front of her. She was arranging them in an order, lining them up very precisely. Doris sat down in the chair beside her, a book laid open where she had been sitting. Trina briefly introduced me to Doris then walked over and said:

"Mother, how are you doing today?"

The woman looked up, big smile, as if she recognized Trina, gave a small laugh and went back to her blocks. Trina touched her hair, putting a strand in place that was on her forehead. She sat down beside her and held her left hand in her right, gently stroking it. She continued to arrange the blocks with her free hand, never looking up.

Trina said: "Did you eat all your lunch today?"

Doris was slowly shaking her head in the negative and her mother looked up at Trina and laughed lightly. Trina said: "I'll be over later to eat dinner with you, ok."

Doris said she had to leave an hour early but that Angie, who I took to be her daughter, would be over by then. Trina sat for five more minutes then gave her a kiss on the head, getting a smile back. Her mother said to Trina, sassily: "The peas are lousy." She went back to her blocks. Trina smiled and gave me a head motion that it was time to go. I told Doris it was nice to meet her and followed Trina back the lane. I walked a step back behind thinking it was one of those moments when someone lets you into a private part of their lives, and you see them part of them for the first time.

We got back to the house and stood in the same place we had just minutes before. I said: "Your mom I take it."

"Good guess. Nancy Meredith Beckett."

"Alzheimer's?"

"That's what some of the doctor's say."

"What do you say?"

"Some men don't physically abuse. They go right for killing the soul. They break so many promises that a person builds a fortress in their mind to survive and stop heartache."

She walked just slightly away from me looking to the ocean, not weakly, but strong, focused, as if reenergized. She said: "Ask me your questions about the Trust. Wasn't that where we were before our walk?"

I sheepishly said: "So is your company really in trouble, or are you just trying to get control of the Trust?"

"So you figured it out. I didn't think it would take you

forever. It makes no difference now. By next week, my father will be out and I will have control of his alter ego."

"So all the government interventions, the IRS, DEP, that's not real."

"Oh, it's real. They are acting like good marionettes, never questioning or caring whose pulling the stings and responding to all the right false information that fits their view of the world. I just set it all in motion."

"You're using the government to destroy your own company?"

"Destroy is rather harsh. They will go away soon, not because of any payoff, or deal, simply because there aren't any facts to support the innuendos and rumors that started all these investigations."

"All with your congressman's help?"

"Jealousy again, Jake? He had nothing to do with it, but I certainly will use him to end it. I cried on his shoulder. As long as our righteous congressman still thinks he can get me into the sack, he'll play along. He'll make a few calls, the files will be looked at, some people will have to justify some actions, which they can't, so apologies will be issued, clearances granted."

"And all the bank ratings will be back in place."

"That will take a few months, but we'll be on the top of the list for government contracts to make up for their behavior."

"All that for what?"

"For what? Do you have a purpose in life Jake?"

God, I hated that philosophical question. What? What? To do good? To be a better person? To pay my taxes? To give blood?

"Honestly, I don't know." I said.

"Most people don't. It's the hollowness of life, isn't it? The moral animal's conscious dilemma. Smarter, but sadder than all those lower animals."

She took a sip of her drink, stirring the ice with her finger. She said: "Did you see my beautiful mother? Alex Beckett did that to her. When I was in my late twenties and really became aware of what he was doing, the purpose started. A purpose doesn't come to someone overnight. It took about the same amount time for me to find my purpose as it did for that bastard to destroy my mother."

"So your purpose is to destroy your father?"

"That's right. However long it takes. Removing him from control of AB Enterprises is a big start."

I looked at her, perplexed, even mystified, by the contrast between the loving daughter and vicious ruthlessness person also inside. I said: "Rather virtuous for you to be the judge and jury. Is that a purpose, settling a score?"

"Don't give me that pious horseshit." Slamming her drink on granite kitchen counter. "I won't wait for a supposedly heavenly 'God' to pass judgment. That god can pass judgment when my father dies. He's living here now and I am passing judgment, just as you would. I'll strip him of the only thing that has meaning to him, his soul, and that's AB Enterprises. And worse, he'll have it done by his daughter. His little girl, his pride and joy and I will tell him right to his face. I was taught by the best. Alex Beckett himself."

"And after you've accomplished that, what?"

"You can ask me then. One purpose in a lifetime should be enough for anyone. You should get one Jake."

I had no response. We stared out at the ocean myself for a quite awhile. Finally I asked her about her mother, her illness, and Trina's care for her. We talked for some time and Trina said she should be getting me back as she needed to help with her mother's dinner. I said I would call a cab, but she insisted on me taking one of her cars. Bring it back tomorrow, she said. And I agreed. At the door on the way out, we almost kissed and almost hugged, but didn't do either. I just gently squeezed her right hand and kissed the top of her head. I said her mother was lucky to have a daughter who loved her so.

I sat in her car in her driveway thinking once again that someone had opened up to me, even if out of anger and I had not reciprocated. Never do. Probably never will. But I realized then I never lost Trina. She was never mine.

Chapter Twenty-Nine

I made my way back toward the Marriott thinking along the way that it was time to have a meeting with Alex. Calling Alex's home and cell, I got no answer, so I called Dean to ask if he knew Alex's whereabouts. He told me more than likely the Boca Health Club working out. He also told me that Alex was taking a late evening helicopter hop over to Cat and would be there a couple days. Dean didn't mention Elizabeth Frampton's death and I didn't bring it up.

When I got to the Marriott I went to the Guest Services computer station off the lobby, checked my email and found Brian had left a message:

Found a picture of Frampton. Surprisingly difficult. None with any publications. No driving records in any state. Finally got the CNI life insurance physical. Don't ask how. Picture attached. Required for physical with doctor. Hope this is helpful.

I pulled up the photo. He appeared to be in his late thirties, square face, short dark curly hair, and weathered complexion. A vaguely familiar face. It was a "line'm up and shot'm" photo, a window on his left and on his right, part of a calendar. Zooming and enlarging the photo, I spotted a handwritten note in the box for the twenty-sixth: *Noon... Junkanoo Parade.* Junkanoo Day was an eighteenth century slave tradition celebrated the day after Christmas and in only one country: the Commonwealth of the Bahamas. The window on his left looked out into a small marina and with the sign on the dock: Cat Cay Club. Printing out the photo, I put it in my wallet, closing out the computer, and then getting directions from the clerk to the Boca Health Club.

The Boca Health Club was on the second floor of an office

building on Sunset Drive. The tread mills facing the all glass front to better see the comings and goings of some of Florida's wealthiest of all ages. Plastic surgeons and Botox made physical appearance unreliable circumstantial evidence of age for Boca residents. Alex was on the bubble for plastic surgery. The health club was his first line of defense.

When I found Alex he had already worked out and was seated at a table by himself, drinking water and reading a magazine. I walked over and he greeted me with his usual enthusiasm, as if expecting me. He said: "Jake, have a seat. Good to see you. Been expecting to hear from you."

I said, glancing at his magazine: "What are you reading?"

"Bonnie told me to read this from Family Circle, 'Why do I attract the wrong type of person?'"

"Why do you?"

"According to this article we attract not what we want, but what we feel we deserve. So basically I must feel I deserve the companionship of unbalanced women. Apparently I feel unworthy of a fulfilling relationship. Low self esteem. I'll have to work on that."

He put the article down and said: "So what's new on helping out the current deranged women in my life?"

I bypassed the small detail of her death and said: "Quite a bit. Hoping maybe you could help me some."

He nodded as I pulled out the photo of Frampton and put it front of him. "Is he alive or dead, Alex?"

He examined the photo and said: "Where'd you get this?"

"Doesn't matter, does it? Yes or no, alive or dead?"

He frowned, suggesting he didn't like my tone, but answered: "If you're asking me about the guy in this photo. He's alive, but this isn't Frampton."

"That's the picture attached to his life insurance policy."

"That doesn't surprise me."

"Well. Who is it?"

He said: "You know him probably. Mike Clontz. First mate for Kamal on the Pharaoh."

"So what's he doing on Frampton's insurance application?"

"Good question."

Getting exasperated at the pace and maybe tired of this old elephant, I said: "What's the fucking answer Alex?"

He narrowed his eyes, but didn't take the fifth, saying: "My guess is Elizabeth had Mike stand in for her husband for the insurance physical by Doctor Leicht when she was at Cat."

"Why'd she do that?"

"Your guess is as good as mine."

"I don't think so." Consciously pushing, I said: "You never get too close to the fire do you Alex?"

He laughed. A condescending laugh. "Got me figured out Jake? I doubt it. I owe some explanations, but not much. I don't take you for naïve. Elizabeth's probably scamming the insurance company and you suspected it from the get go."

"So why put me in that position Alex? Act as your canary?"

"Not really. I knew they would pay. You might as well get the business as anyone else. But yeah. You're the ethical one in our pool. Face it Jake, you usually won't go the distance. You love your status quo. That's why your career went no where. If it got too crazy, you pulling out would be the first sign for me."

He was right about the career and he knew I knew it. I shot back: "Sign that your own stock scam might be in jeopardy?"

"That's good Jake. Your weasel Bryan's been hard at work. The stock offering. Ovonics. No scam. Unless you consider all of Wall Street a scam, which maybe it is. I read all of George Frampton's articles, the research, nano-stuff. Corning was on board, so Elizabeth said. Some government interest too. That never hurts the price."

"What about your friend Bert Tad getting killed, was that factored in?"

"No." The tone at first somber, then briskly: "I had nothing to do with that. Maybe you should ask Elizabeth what she knows about that."

Since everyone seemed to be lying, I thought I would join in: "She said for me to ask you where her palm pilot is."

"The palm pilot. I have no idea. If you mean the Corning palm pilot, I told her that was going to be nothing but trouble. She should give it back. She said it was her insurance. Whatever that meant."

"I guess the extra million of insurance wasn't enough."

His look was truly one of surprise. He said, grinning: "Son of a bitch. You got to give her credit. Didn't know about that."

"Always keeping enough distance so you wouldn't get drawn in too deep?"

He smiled again. A tacit acknowledgement of his character. Slicks or slobs commit crimes. He was no slob. He said: "Like I said, ask your client where the palm pilot is."

I figured now was a good time as any. I said: "Can't do that now."

With a quizzical look he said: "She fired you? Without telling me. That surprises me."

"I guess it surprises you that she's dead too."

Not shocked. Not surprised. Which maybe that was a reaction in itself. Simply another fact for Alex to quickly assimilate. He said expressionless: "When? How?" Same as Trina. Appeared genuine. Just like her.

"Last night. Probably bludgeoned to death. Know anything about it?"

"Nothing. I swear to god. Listen, Jake. I'll push the envelope in the money game. But that's all it is. A game. I had nothing to do with her death."

"I want to believe you Alex. But whether I do doesn't matter. Whether Sheriff McManus does is another story."

"He knows I wouldn't be involved in something like that."

"He'd like to believe that. We're back to my original question. I'll put it another way: Did you and Elizabeth send Mr. Frampton to the bottom of the ocean?"

"No. Her angle in the beginning was the insurance. From what I could tell, she planned the whole lost at sea routine. In fact, I was pissed about my fucking boat going to the bottom. I spent a lot of time designing that one."

"How'd she do it?"

"I don't know. Cold cash, my bet. Probably her and Mike. Doug and I figured that one of the drug runners helped them and they would put it down on the ledge. Amateur mistake involving someone else. Probably the guys who helped were the ones who shot at you and OB coming back from Bimini. I don't know for sure. Believe me."

I didn't. I said: "So when you hired Doug to find the boat he already knew where to look."

"Pretty much." He started to get up and said: "I've got go. I'm flying over to Cat tonight. Christ, Elizabeth is dead. Who do you think did it?"

"Don't know. Same people who maybe killed Tad? You should think about that." I said.

"You're welcome to go along to Cat with me, Jake. I'll answer whatever else I can."

I think he thought he genuinely meant it too. I got up with him and on the way out I said: "Have you got your notice about the Trust Meeting yet?"

"Yeah. That's Trina's game. I don't know why she just didn't ask. I'd be glad to turn it all over to her. She runs ABE better than I ever did."

I said: "Maybe she has something to prove." Giving him an opening.

"You think I don't know she holds me responsible for her mother. There's two sides to every story."

"Maybe she needs to hear your side."

"Maybe she does. But she won't. That's between her mother and me. I honor that to my grave."

Honor seemed an odd choice of words. I said: "One more thing you ought to know. Your daughter's one of the suspects in Frampton's murder."

"That's impossible."

"Maybe so, but they can put her at the scene, her prints are probably all over the apartment, and they'll put together a motive eventually."

"Which is?"

"Protecting dad."

He didn't respond. I said: "One last time Alex. Do you know if Elizabeth Frampton's husband is alive?"

"Jake you got three choices. One, he's alive and up to no good. Two, he's dead and not our concern anymore. Or a third."

"What's that?"

Just before he shut his car door he answered: "The third choice. Isn't it obvious: he never existed."

Chapter Thirty

The traffic on Interstate I-95 south was light but fast toward Pompano. I pondered whether the dog in me had any fight left. It might be better to stay on the porch. As I turned off I-95 my cell rang without a caller id number. I flipped it open, hearing: "Mister Quinn."

Not recognizing the voice, I said: "That's right. Who's this?"

"Trina Beckett still safe?"

Uncertain thoughts, I said: "Like I said, who is this?"

"You don't need to know. What you do need to do is turn over the Corning Palm Pilot to me."

No face to the voice. The implicit threat to Trina unsettling. Fighting anger, I said: "I think I'll hang on to it for awhile."

"The pilot's not yours to keep. Only more people can get hurt if you don't."

I decided to take a shot at what I suspected: "Like your wife Elizabeth?"

No change in voice, he said: "You're way out of your league. If you're stupid enough to not care about yourself, you might want to think of a few people around you. I already mentioned one."

The threat only swelled my antagonism at this coward and with forced control I said: "Where do I meet you?"

"You don't want to do that. Leave it in your motel room tonight and check out."

Sarcastically I said: "You know, I think I left it over at Cat Cay."

Now with his own anger, he said: "Don't fuck with me Quinn."

"You shouldn't have called me by my last name. I'll see you

at Cat." I pressed "End", then quickly speed dialed Trina. Before I could say anything she answered pleasantly: "Couldn't stay away?"

I said abruptly: "Listen. You're in danger. Lock the doors. Turn on all the outside lights. Find a safe room."

She knew I wasn't kidding. She said: "What's going on?"

"I don't know. I'm on my way over."

She said all right. I hung up and worked my way through the fast and furious drivers of southern Florida to Trina's. When I squealed into her driveway the house lights were on all around. I dialed Trina's cell. She answered and said she felt stupid sitting in her bathroom with a shotgun on her lap. I wonder myself if I was overreacting. I told her to open the front door, quickly. Letting me in, I pushed her to the hallway, out of line of the windows.

"What's this all about?" She demanded.

"I don't know everything but I need to get you to some place safe."

"Come on. That's not enough. We're going nowhere until you tell me who's after you and why the panic."

"I don't know who it is, maybe Frampton. But I know what they're after and that's the palm pilot Frampton took from Corning. I have it now and they want it. And I don't want them using you as a hostage."

"Where is it?"

"It's behind the bar at Parkers."

"Let's get it." She said.

"I planned on that but that plan does not include you."

"It does now."

Actually, it made more sense for her to go with me and arguing would not do any good anyway. I said: "All right. Get whatever you're going to take and I'll wait here."

She opened her palms in a gesture of having everything she needed on her and said: "Let's go. I already called Doris and she took my mom over to her house."

We quickly got outside and jumped in her BMW, Trina driving as she knew the quickest back way to Parkers. The plan to get the pilot, which Lou allowed me to hide at the bar the day

166

Frampton gave it to me, was not sophisticated. Avoiding the front entrance, Trina would park near the alley behind Parkers and I would go in through the back. Once I had the pilot we would think about where to spend the evening and then probably head over to cat.

Pulling into the alley within sight of the back door, I got out, walked down the alley, through the unlocked kitchen door and into the bar area. Mo saw me and said: "Did I see you come in?"

I went over to her and said outside of the ear shot of several patrons: "I left something behind the bar last time in, I need to get it."

She said: "Be my guest."

Walking around behind the bar I took the pickled egg jar off the counter and put it on the bar sink. I opened the lid and took the tongs and worked my way to the middle of the purple elixir, pulled out a small package wrapped with plastic and duck tape. Mo, seeing this, said: "Lou kept telling me not to sell any eggs. I almost threw the whole container out today figuring they were spoiled."

With that I was thinking I was not that clever. It took a few moments to dry it off and undo the tape and plastic. I said to Mo: "I owe you then."

She said: "I'm going to collect on that someday."

I said melodramatically: "Hope I'm around to give you the chance."

I put the dry pilot in my pocket and headed out through the kitchen to the back door. Opening the screen door, I stepped into the alley when suddenly I was pushed and slammed forward into a collection of garbage and junk. Before I could right myself someone was coming at me, not quickly, but steadily, and said: "Turn it over, right now."

In the darkness I couldn't see if he was coming at me with a gun or not. Laying there I waited a second until he was closer, and then swung my legs into his feet, kicking them out from under him, dropping him quickly on his hip, the pistol that was in his hand, hitting the pavement. He quickly got up and I swung hard with my fist into his stomach, causing him to hunch over, dropping to his knees. Down on his knees holding his stomach, I crouched down in front of him to check his pockets for another weapon and said: "Frampton?"

His face was still distorted and he began to look up at me when Mo, who must have heard the commotion, came into the alley wielding a baseball bat. I said to her: "Hold this asshole."

She had her foot on his back, picked up the pistol and said: "Gladly."

I didn't see Trina's BMW and ran down the alley where she should have been parked. I saw her taillights several blocks ahead and started running in that direction but they faded quickly from sight. My cell rang. I stopped and flipped it open. The voice, now familiar, said:

"You seem not to value your life Quinn. But we have something of value to exchange now. Don't take too long getting to Cat. My patience is wearing thin."

He hung up this time. My cleverness was catching up with me and overtaking others. I needed someone to send me an angel. A big nasty one and god damn smart too.

Chapter Thirty-One

———

I ran back down the alley. Mo motioned me inside to an office area where she had our man in a chair with his arms tied behind him, movie style. Short, overweight, resembling a Daily News reporter out of a Mickie Spillane novel. His wallet was on the table and I picked it up. I had no idea who he was but figured he was involved in the set up with whoever had Trina.

He said matter of factly: "Kidnapping's a felony you know, even in this redneck state."

Ignoring him, I checked the cards in his wallet. He wasn't George Frampton, but I knew by now it wouldn't be. His driver's license read: Harold Kenjerlak, Jr., Buffalo, New York, age 51. He had numerous credit cards and a private investigator's license for Great State of New York. There was a small note pad, and although I could barely read his writings, there were notes tracking my comings and goings the last few days. He said, apparently impatient: "I'm serious. Let me go."

Dawning on me that this cracker almost got me killed, and maybe did or will get Trina killed, I said: "Why don't you shut the fuck up before I beat the shit out of you."

"Lot of good that will do you." Said in a sarcastic tone, to which, to my own surprise, I responded by smacking him hard across his face with the back of my hand. Mo's glanced at me with an acknowledged look of approval.

His shaken look bared no tough guy, saying, now in a pleading tone: "I got nothing to hide, what do you want to know?"

"Let's start with how long you've been following me?"

"Just since you've been down here in Florida. It's a freelance job. For iJet. I do work for them on occasion. Ones where they want results. No reports. I don't know who hired them. I was told it was corporate espionage. You and the Frampton women were to be followed. Said you had some corporate material is all. They wanted it back."

"So why'd you jump me?"

"I was waiting here at Parkers for you. Most people follow a pattern. You're no different. I figured you'd show up tonight eventually. You walked in through the back. I saw you get whatever is in the stupid egg jar. Decided to take a shot."

It made sense, if anything did right now. I said: "So what do you know about Trina Beckett?"

"I don't know anything about her, other than she picked you up earlier at her business in Pompano."

"What about Bert Tad?"

"Who?" Said with enough of a quizzical face to be believed.

"Were you following Elizabeth Frampton?"

"Not really."

The hesitancy in the response was just enough to set me off, but before I could react, Mo had smashed her small but strong fist into his rib cage. He doubled over, her saying: "Perhaps you think we give a shit about you. Or that we wouldn't dump your sorry Buffalo ass in the ocean."

No immediate response, as he couldn't catch his breath from the obvious pain. He finally said: "I staked out her apartment after you left here. A man goes in. Looked like he had a key. I don't know. I fall asleep and then leave. The next day the sheriff's people are all over the place. I heard she was dead. I swear it's the truth. Check my notes there."

"What about George Frampton? Had she been with him?"

"Like I said, I don't know much about the Framptons. I was told he might be alive, might not. To keep an eye out. They gave me a picture. It's in the wallet. I think that's the guy who I saw go into the apartment. It was dark."

He was nodding with his head toward the desk where his wallet contents were laid out. There were wallet size digital pictures of me, Elizabeth Frampton and a third one. I picked it up and showed it to him.

"That's the guy they said was Frampton. He's the one I

thought I saw go into the apartment."

I said: "You can tell all that to the Sheriff."

He slumped further down in the chair. I pulled Mo aside and told her I didn't have time to wait for the Sheriff and to keep him here for the night then call the Sheriff to pick him up. I put the picture in my pocket.

Mo loaned me her car to get back to the Marriott saying she would pick it up later. Dealing with the iJet dick took my mind temporarily off Trina's fate but I counted on Trina's captor thinking there was no hope in getting the pilot without her being healthy. With that I had some time, but not much. It did me no good to get over to Cat Cay at night, armed or unarmed. I needed some help. On the way back to the motel, I phoned Diane, who answered, with a worried mother-like tone: "How are you?"

I said quickly: "Fine. Diane, I need a favor."

"What do you need?"

"I need to be certain I have a seat on the early Island Air flight tomorrow to Cat Cay out of Lauderdale."

"I'm sure that I can set that up."

Before she said anything more I said: "I need to be certain that my carry-on is not checked."

"That may be difficult."

I said with some harshness: "If all this clandestine activity you and Bert Tad were involved in is true, then it shouldn't be too tall an order."

"I'll see what I can do. You need to know we have more information on Mr. Tad's death. Homeland Security or a Pentagon team was trying to shake down Tad for information about Cat. They wanted information on the palm pilot that Frampton had. All the teams have been called in but it's true what you were told: one is still out there. Either he hasn't been found and told to come in or he's on a mission of his own. Getting you killed was not what I had in mind Jake. I am sending someone but you need to wait. He needs time to get there."

"Thanks, but that's not necessary."

"You have to understand these guys are cloaked, even a

rogue acting on his own."

"What the hell does that mean?"

"They're immune from prosecution."

"I'll keep that in mind."

She said: "Jake. I'm serious. Please. Wait."

I said, clicking off: "I'm beyond waiting."

When I got back to my room I pulled the photo out of my pocket. In a navy uniform, the universal submariners insignia, Neptune rising, on his shirt, the face matched the one I already had and that Alex confirmed: Kamil's first mate, Mike Clontz.

Chapter Thirty-Two

——

Island Air's first flight to Cat Cay, weather permitting, was scheduled for 7:25 am. I arrived at Fort Lauderdale International at 6:30 am, on only a few hours of restless sleep. Diane had left a voice mail that I was to take what I wanted in a black leather travel bag to be purchased at Travel Smith just inside the terminal. The clerk already knew the arrangement. I purchased the bag, went to the restroom, put my ankle Glock and some clothes inside, throwing my original bag in the garbage.

I walked to the Island Air desk just off Signature's small terminal near the runway. Identifying myself to the ticket clerk, I was told that a seat had been arranged, the hop was leaving on time and I was the only passenger. She pointed me to the security entrance. I didn't know what Diane had arranged if anything, but I showed no outward sign of hesitation and thanked her.

Just before rounding the corridor to the TSA Security Check point, pilot Cliff Cox came up to me with a loud greeting. "Jake Quinn. Ready to fly."

"Sure. Cliff."

He said, no hesitation: "Let me check that for weight. We're loaded for bear today."

I handed him the bag as he put the bag he was carrying, identical black leather, on the floor next to mine, leaning down as if checking mine. He got up taking mine, handing me his, and we walked to the check point. He had in his right hand a fishing rod with a large metal spinning reel attached. As we approached the guards, Cliff said to me: "Check'er through. I'll meet you on the other side."

Cliff walked ahead casually passing through the metal

detector, bantering with the security, which he saw at least six to eight times a day depending on flights. The buzzer sounded he walked through with my bag. He smiled and was waived through. I put my new bag through the screener and waited while it was stopped and scanned. I was waived through.

Walking to the plane Cliff pointed to the passenger side door. I climbed in. The plane was full of cases of Guinness, Harp and assorted wines. He finished his walk around, got in and pointed for me to put on the passenger head set. We taxied out and were in the air shortly.

As we banked over the Atlantic I had unorganized dark thoughts about Trina. Adrenaline either feeds or blocks emotion. I struggled to flip my numbing fear into rational hatred of her captor. Logic alone was not going to get me through this. I thought of what it must be like to be a soldier behind enemy lines, untrained for the mission.

As we approached Cat I saw several boats in the cove at the entrance and numerous fifty foot yachts in the dock area. I noticed one sail boat off South Cat Island. We landed, got out and Cliff handed me my bag. We golf carted to the custom shed while outbound passengers stood by. I was checked through and Cliff said: "I put a Kevlar bullet proof vest in your bag."

"Tell Diane I said thanks."

He said: "Don't know Diane or what this is about. Don't want to. Hope you know what you're doing. Good luck. Jake."

I walked down the sidewalk in front of the docks which led past the restaurant to Boo's Bar. When I got to Boo's Bar Leland was cleaning glasses and getting ready for the day. I walked up and sat down. He said:

"Ah. Mister Quinn. So good to see you. Iced tea. No sweet. No lemon."

"Hi. Leland. Thanks. That'd be great."

As he slid tea in front of me, I put down the plastic raised Duke of Windsor stamp, making sure he saw it. I said: "I need some help Leland."

He picked the stamp up and placed it in the palm of his hand, casually glancing around, making sure no one was within ear shot. His expression changed, no longer the humble colonial

Bahamian servant, more the hard look when ordering the staff around. No island cadence. He said: "What do you want to know?"

"What do I need to know?"

"Mike Clontz was found dead last night on the beach cove near Alex Beckett's house. Beat'n to death."

"Do they know who did it?"

"If you mean they, as customs or the local police, no. They're trying to make sure the killer's not one of the locals who work here. They'll start questioning the residents soon, but they have to be careful with that. Clontz was a nobody as far they're concerned. They want it to just go away. Classified as a body that washed ashore. Happens several times a year. Turn it over to the Americans in Miami."

"What do you think?"

"Alex showed up at Kirkland's late last night. He was a mess. Bloody face from some cuts. Probably some broken ribs. Asked her to patch him up. She did and he told her not to say anything. He said he fell off his boat, bone fishing in the flats. Gave her a couple hundred in cash to be quiet. Said he was taking the helicopter out of here today. He hasn't left yet."

"Have you seen Trina?" I said.

"No."

"Any new boats come in the dock?"

"Off shore at South Cat. Same one we see here about once a week."

I didn't know what else to ask and I needed to get up to Alex's before he left. One of the waiters was coming by. I said thanks and told Leland I was going up to Alex's. He said quickly: "I'm told someone is coming over to help you. Don't do anything stupid Jake."

The waiter was close by. I said: "Thanks for the tea Leland."

He said, accent back: "No problem, mon."

Heading up the path to Alex's house, I felt a sense of urgency. I went around back to the patio, seeing Alex sitting on the couch with his legs up. I walked in seeing he had a bandage on his forehead, his right hand was wrapped, and an open shirt

175

so you could see the wrap around his ribs. He didn't get up. Smiling he said:

"Jake. Come on in. Had a little boating accident. Damn unstable flat boats. What's up?"

Amazing. Couldn't he lie any better? I said: "Alex, I truly don't have time for bullshit. What happened to Mike Clontz?"

"Clontz. Yeah, that's something. How about him washing up on shore? I guess they'll be asking a lot of questions about that. I'm heading back today. If you're sticking around maybe you could tell them to get a hold of me next week. You could find out what's going on."

In a quick angry tone I said: "Alex. Your games are beyond me. I'm over here because I'm looking for Trina. Somebody has her and is using her as bait to get the fucking palm pilot you and Frampton won't give back. If you give a shit about your daughter, tell me right now what's going on. If you don't then I'll fucking beat it out of you."

I don't know if it was the threat or concern about Trina, but he said: "I killed Clontz. He came in here last night, threatening me, saying he was going to the authorities about me and Elizabeth. He and her were in on sinking the boat. I had nothing to do with it. He was supposed to be in for twenty-five per cent of whatever she got. He found out she was leaving town with all the money. He said he killed her in an argument then set it up to look like an accident. Said he saw Trina there right before him and if I didn't come up with some money, his share, he was going to pin the murder on Trina. I don't know who's telling the truth. I told him to do what he wants. He starts to walk out. I grabbed him and there's a struggle. I hit him with a conch shell. It was him or me. Fuck'm."

"What'd you do with the body?"

"I dumped it out on the flats. I looked around here and found some jewelry of Elizabeth's and put it in his pocket with a bunch of cash. Sheriff McDonald will figure out the rest."

"Just like that."

"Fucking just like that. I don't know if he killed Elizabeth or not. Maybe Trina actually did. I'm not taking that chance."

"Who has Trina? George Frampton?"

"Don't you get it? Didn't you figure it out? There is no Frampton. He never existed. Elizabeth made the whole thing up. Son of bitch, Jake, we have to find Trina."

He started to get up but flinched from the pain. My cell phone rang. I answered. The voice said: "You're wasting time talking to dad. Bring the pilot over to South Cat now and she goes free." He clicked off.

Alex said: "Who was that?"

Ignoring the question, I said: "Where's your runabout?"

"Down below in the cove. Damn it Jake, you got to get her out of this. Whatever I have, he can have. Any amount of money."

"You can't buy your way out of this one Alex."

He had his head down now, swearing and mumbling to himself. I left running down to the runabout in the cove. I pushed it off into the water, turned it around and headed out, full throttle toward South Cat.

Give up the pilot and get the girl in exchange. No more cleverness. Real simple now. Trina would be proud of me. I had a purpose in life.

Chapter Thirty-Three

———

The runabout was wide open as I rammed it on the shore of South Cat. No need for a quiet entrance. He knew I was coming. No more illusion that I was dealing with a bumbling husband. There was only one conclusion: this was the rogue I had been warned about. I took the calculated risk he would not want to kill me until he was sure I had the palm pilot. Jumping out of the runabout, I started through an opening in the thicket. South Cat had been abandoned fifty or more years ago, the docks gone, the island all but unwalkable, thick brush and cutting thorns reclaiming her natural state.

The stone lighthouse was fifty yards ahead, the caretaker's roofless home and abandoned windowless walls on my left. Approaching the walls, he yelled out from above: "That's far enough."

I stepped behind one of the walls of house, still with a view of the top of the lighthouse where the voice came from. Overpowering him was not an option. His training was in combat. Stealth. Mine in argument. Persuasion.

I said: "Let me hear Trina say she's ok."

A few seconds then Trina: "I'm alright Jake." Her voice clear, but the tone unsure.

"Happy now."

Thinking what Alex had just confirmed, I said: "Listen. You're chasing a ghost. George Frampton never existed. It was a scam. The palm pilot's worthless."

"Ok. All the more reason for you to hand it over and save her life. I don't want to kill either of you."

Obviously wrong about my ability to persuade, this was no way to start hostage negotiations. I said: "Is killing innocent people and deciding who lives part of your training?"

"You fool. I don't decide. You do. I follow orders. Do you think I am operating on my own? The American people expect it and we're doing it."

"And killing Bert Tad, that was part of your mission?"

"We didn't kill Tad, Tad killed himself. He couldn't leave well enough alone. The team tried to reason with him. We warned him to leave it alone. The old man put up too much of struggle. ."

"Your teams were called home. Your mission's been aborted"

There was a long pause.

He said: "It's over when I say it's over. No sooner. Now turn over the fucking pilot, before I have to kill this woman. The bloods on your hands, not mine."

Trina yelled: "Get out of here Jake. He's going to kill us anyway."

I heard him slap her, and her cry out. I walked out into the open, both hands in the air, pilot in my left hand, high: "Here's the pilot."

He said: "I'm coming down and bringing her with me. Don't do anything stupid."

He came down the steps with Trina ahead of him, her hands tied in front of her. He walked over, with a gun in his right hand and Trina's upper arm grasped by his left. He looked at me and said: "Hand it over."

"It's not going to do you any good without the code."

"The whole point was to get the pilot out of circulation. We could care less about the code."

He walked further toward me as I was still holding the pilot high in the air. I said: "How do you know I'm giving you the right pilot?"

He stopped. Staring at me, then smiling, putting the gun to Trina's head, he said: "That's why she's coming with me, until we find out."

I said: "It's the right one. Catch."

I tossed the pilot just to his left, slightly in front of Trina so his natural instinct was to try to catch it. He lunged, letting go of Trina's arm as I yelled: "Run Trina. I'll take care of this fucking coward!"

She turned and ran down the path behind her, around the other side of the lighthouse. I turned and started to run in the opposite direction, but still in his direct sight. Running with my head down, but not too fast, hoping he would follow me, not Trina, equally hopeful that whatever vest Diane arranged for me would stop the bullet coming my way. A split second later the sound and impact were simultaneous. It felt like a sledgehammer had hit my back, flipping me to the ground. I was knocked into a bush, tangled, partly hidden, on my side, feeling as though my whole shoulder was gone. He was walking toward me. I had my hand down to my ankle and my Glock out from its holster. I was starting to spin, passing out, but I could see a figure. My hand shook. I aimed in his direction and pulled the trigger: once, twice, three times…. My arm fell to the ground. I lay staring at the sky. Unable to move.

I don't know how long I laid there. I saw Trina's face staring down at me. Real or unreal. I didn't know. Dark waves came over me. The last vision before passing out was Trina lips moving. She said: "Lay still. I'm going for help."

Epilogue

S tillwater River, Montana. Earlier in the week I was standing on a street corner in Red Lodge, Montana. A bronze plaque on a building I leaned against read: "The Sundance Kid of the Hole in the Wall Gang robbed this Bank in 1896." I had been waiting for Wanda who was picking me up to meet my riding partner, Dan, for a horseback trip into Custer National Forest. She picked me up in her 250 Diesel Ram with cow horns attached to the front. Wanda and Tiny, her cowboy husband, and their two dogs led us later that day on the horseback ride, mules in tow, up the narrow trail along the descending Stillwater River, racing hundreds of feet below us. Mount Douglas on one side, Granite Peak and the great Beartooth Highway on the other. At various points on the trail, Tiny was quite pleased with himself, singing portions of the Beatle's Rocky Rocco: *"She and her man, who called himself Dan, were in the next room at the hoedown..."*

Our camp was along the calm and tranquil upper Stillwater, the same Stillwater where Butch and Sundance made an escape or two. I sat on a large boulder protruding into the Stillwater, watching a young hawk learning his trade. I closed my eyes and wondered if any of the Hole in the Wall gang had sat on the same boulder, avoiding thoughts of what the future held, as I seemed to be doing.

I tried lying down on the boulder, seeking that body contour that fits sometimes on such rocks, but my shoulder was still sore. The Kevlar vest stopped penetration as designed, but the blunt force impact was traumatic. They told me the shooter was using non-lethal bullets, but you couldn't prove it by me, other than the fact I was alive.

Over the past two months I'd had plenty of time to ponder, as they say, a "near death experience." The first week after Cat Cay was spent in Fort Lauderdale Memorial Hospital, after that back in Pennsylvania, first week on the couch above the office. Slowly over the weeks I worked to a full practice, Eva helping me back to the good graces of the law, supported by superbly boring real estate closings and mundane probate filings. Along the way a few fishing excursions with Moot, and a visit to Zero, whose charges were dropped. Zero continues to try to obtain information on anyone else involved with the death of Bert Tad but is realizing all those doors are shut.

Dean called earlier in the month to tell me that he and Trina, who now controlled all of A.B.E., had reached an agreement on his purchase of the Pompano Beach complex. I would be drawing up the papers. He said Bonnie would email the terms Trina dictated, but before I left for Montana and Wyoming, I hadn't received them.

Dean told me the Bahamian authorities closed the book on the death of Mike Clontz. No mention of Alex, just another body washing up on shore. Alex made sure the report listed the jewelry he planted on Clontz, his insurance policy if anyone in his family was linked to the death of Elizabeth Frampton. Elizabeth Frampton had become another Florida death statistic. Sheriff McDonald listed her death as accidental. In a conversation with Trina last month the sheriff wanted her to know there were no fingerprints found and no eyewitnesses. But he could not "officially" close the file for eighteen months, as the evidence on a possible killer might show up. Those eighteen months happened to be the same time frame for his reelection, giving Alex and Trina plenty of time for campaign contributions and perhaps a yacht club fund raiser or two.

Alex had asked me to assist some of his big guns in settling up on the Morgan Stanley lawsuit that was just starting to brew, but I passed. He had been offered just under five million dollars in a quick settlement. With Elizabeth Frampton dead and George Frampton presumed dead, Morgan/Stanley had nothing to take into court to prove any wrongdoing by Alex. He turned them down, demanding twenty, a bargain according to Alex. That was until three weeks ago when the real "George

Frampton", whose name was "Rob Combs" did indeed turn up to collect the body of his wife and fly it back to England for burial. He was an airline pilot with British Airways and they had been separated for several years. He had known nothing about her activities or even whereabouts. Ironically, CNI was stuck with their iron clad release with Elizabeth Frampton and the real George Frampton will get to keep the one hundred thousand already paid as he is the only beneficiary of her estate. Eva had sent a bill to the estate for our services while representing her, and he paid it within the week.

I looked back over to camp and Wanda and her dogs were still laying under the pines, the horses semi circled nearby, attached to a rope line strung between the trees. Tiny had gone back down the trail to pick up another rider and lead her back to our camp. My riding partner was getting ready to take a half day ride on his own up to the head waters of Stillwater. He looked like a real cowboy, just as he looked the part of Harley dude back at Parkers, and the Naval Academy graduate in the picture Diane showed me at the Gettysburg.

Before he left I had helped him saddle up and thanked him for inviting me. I also asked him a question that had been haunting me: who it was I killed? It turns out I killed no one. On instructions from Diane, Dan had arrived on South Cat shortly after I did. He was waiting to see if the rogue was going to let Trina and I go, before he moved in. He was under orders to subdue the rogue and bring him back in, which he was about to do when I threw the pilot and starting running. He could not shoot as I was in his line of fire. When the rogue shot me, he waited until he came over close enough to take him hand to hand. When I was lying on the ground and started wildly firing, he had no choice but to put the rogue down with a stunning bullet. He guessed correctly that the rogue did not intend on killing me or Trina as he had confirmed Tad's death had indeed been an accident in a struggle with other members of the rogue's team. He stayed hidden until Trina left for help, and then took the rogue off Cat. Apparently the government is still trying to figure out what to do with him.

I had thanked him for saving my life but he told me to thank his mother. I had never made the connection from the first photo Diane showed me of him at Annapolis. Diane was right that there was much more I needed to know about her and Tad Industries. Particularly if I was going to work for them as Diane proposed.

I watched Dan head up the Stillwater trail. I laid back on the boulder, watching the hawk start to get it right, wondering if the next time I would. I heard Tiny coming back up the trail with our last rider. Soon I heard a rustle behind me, someone crawling up on my rock, sitting beside me. She didn't say a word. We smiled at each other, enjoying the solitude, leaning against each other. I couldn't tell if she was holding me up or I her. I drifted off for a moment remembering the lyrics to a song playing on the radio on our ride from Red Lodge:

You've got to find somebody to love you
Someone to be there for you night and day
Someone to share it with and be part of you
Love ain't no good 'till you give it away

You're gonna find out sooner or later
You need a common denominator

When I woke up, we were still together on the boulder, my head on her lap, looking up at Diane's smiling face.

I said, smiling: "And your name is?"

"You're gonna find out sooner or later."

"Aren't you the one that owes me twenty-five thousand?"

"You want paid now?"

"We have plenty of time to work out the denominations." I said.

Diane said: "We can find out what we have in common, if you have the guts. But I have to tell you, it's the uncommon parts that make it work."

Sitting there the longest time, I said, breaking the silence: "I feel like I've waited my whole lifetime for a moment of truth."

She didn't say anything as I stared at the pool of clear water surrounding us.

"I wonder how deep it is." I said.
She said: "Sometimes it takes a leap of faith."
I grinned, stood up and jumped in.

Printed in the United States
38863LVS00007B/159

9 781932 672466